KINGDOM OF DUST

Also by
Lisa Stringfellow

A Comb of Wishes

KINGDOM
OF
DUST

LISA STRINGFELLOW

Quill Tree Books
An Imprint of HarperCollinsPublishers

Quill Tree Books is an imprint of HarperCollins Publishers.

Kingdom of Dust
Copyright © 2024 by Lisa Stringfellow
All rights reserved. Printed in the United States of America.
No part of this book may be used or reproduced in any manner
whatsoever without written permission except in the case of
brief quotations embodied in critical articles and reviews. For
information address HarperCollins Children's Books, a division of
HarperCollins Publishers, 195 Broadway, New York, NY 10007.
www.harpercollinschildrens.com

Library of Congress Control Number: 2023944484
ISBN 978-0-06-304348-0

Typography by David Curtis
24 25 26 27 28 LBC 5 4 3 2 1
First Edition

To the griots of my family,
who have kept alive memories and
bravely forged paths for me to follow.

When a griot dies, it is as if a library
has burned to the ground.
—*West African proverb*

Contents

CHAPTER 1

PRAISE SONG
FOR KUN

O Kun
Motherland of grass and sun
Oala blesses us

Where the Eke River flows
Through plains and soaring mountains
Red clay of her heart

From hot sands of the Zare
To bright and azure seas
Cradle of the goddess

From her we are born
To her we shall return
Her children, one and all

O Kun
Remember the goddess
Forsake not her blessings

In our past
One reads our future

O Kun
Do not forget

—Sung by Griot Kelechi to Eze Ikemba on his coronation, Kingdom of Kun

CHAPTER 2

HOPE AND HUNGER

Dust clings to my feet with every step across the barren yard. I drop the frayed basket into the back of the cart with a thump and pick up one of the yams cradled inside. The last of our harvest, it is covered with the same grit that scrapes between my toes. I gently rub its bristly fibers with the worn edge of my skirt. It helps, but dust settles again, making it look as if I have just pulled it from the ground.

I push the basket farther into the cart and wedge it next to the pile of star apples. Lines of sticky perspiration tickle my skin, and my cornrows itch as I walk over to scratch Mango behind his ears. The donkey makes a soft snort and puts his face close to mine. Hot breath tickles the skin above the crescent-shaped birthmark on my neck. His warm muzzle feels like a kiss on my cheek.

Over in our mud brick house, Zirachi kneels in silent prayer before our two household altars.

It is said in Kun that you can't know who you are unless you can call the names of your ancestors going back seven generations. The altar for Zirachi's family holds her grandmother's cowrie shell necklace and a knife her great-grandfather favored. Such tokens are necessary to recall, honor, and seek wisdom from our relatives. I shuffle my feet.

I could honor Zirachi's ancestors, but who am I if I can't name my own?

Cushioned by the dust, I pad silently to the doorway and listen.

"Oala," Zirachi whispers, "bless our efforts today." She places a plump star apple, sweet and tart, on an altar for Oala—Kun's great and beautiful goddess of creation. A sculpted python coils in restful sleep among dried flowers and other gifts. The little serpent offers protection to our home and relays our messages to the goddess.

When she finishes with her prayers, Zirachi raises herself from the altars and notices me.

"Come along, Amara," she says. "It's time."

In the yard, she adjusts the harnesses on Mango.

The sky blooms orange above us, hazy clouds mirroring the dust that swallows our feet.

"I hope Oala sends us rain," I say. Hopping up to the rough cart seat, I brush more sandy grit from my skirt.

"As do I," Zirachi says with a sigh. "Pray that it may stop the Zare's hunger."

I have no memory of a time before the Zare, the great desert, devoured our land. Zirachi tells me stories of when Kun had lush, green fields and fat cattle. From the desert to the sea, there was always plenty. Now even she has trouble remembering the way it was.

When we finally reach the little village of Danel, crowds throng the paths. My heart jumps, and hope creeps into Zirachi's eyes.

"There are more people today," I say. "Are they here for the New Yam Festival tomorrow?"

Zirachi glances among the bright awnings and tent poles in the village square. "It must be so," she replies.

We carry our offering to the temple. I can't balance the heavy basket of new yams on my head as well as Zirachi, but I manage without dropping it.

The courtyard is busy with preparations for

tomorrow's festival. The elders direct where the tributes should be placed. Groups of men and women prepare the colorful costumes and headpieces that the masquerade dancers will don. A dancer wearing a leopard mask practices his steps to the drum.

"I pray that fortune changes," Zirachi says.

"And that we have fresh yams to eat again," I mutter. "Why did we give away so many?"

Zirachi sighs. "Amara, it's tradition. The festival marks the end of one harvest and the beginning of the next. We celebrate not just what we have, but what we hope for," she says. "Only one more day, little one, then we can eat what we have grown. Besides, I hear the Eze himself may be present."

"In Danel?" I ask incredulously. I have never seen the king and wonder why he would come to a village such as ours.

"Yes. And you should not speak so frivolously. We have little, but some have none. Let's be grateful."

I nod, knowing that Zirachi speaks the truth. We pass under the twisted branches of a large star apple tree, and I remember trying to wrap my arms around its gnarled trunk when I was little.

No star apples fall now. Even at season's end, the tree holds tight to its fruit, desperate to keep every drop of moisture. Desiccated star apples rattle on the branches. The people hunger, but the tree gives nothing.

After leaving our harvest gifts at the temple, we return to the cart to carry the rest of our wares to our usual spot in the market. New yams cannot be sold until after the festival, and we must sell what we have left or throw them away. We cannot afford to let any return to the dust.

Shrill voices from nearby stalls compete for the attention of the marketgoers. *Here! Here! Come!*

"Amara"—Zirachi's eyes scan the crowd—"I am going to see Mmesoma across the way. Keep your eyes sharp, and do not leave the mat. We mustn't lose what we have to a thief's quick hand." Her voice is direct, but not harsh.

"I will." Zirachi's amber eyes, so unlike my brown ones, crinkle slightly and she gives my shoulder a firm squeeze before she strides off.

"Yams! Star apples!" I call. In a few moments, I see Chigozie approach, and I smile. One of our regular customers, she says her husband likes our yams best, and we try to save our fattest ones for her each week. "Good morning, Auntie," I say.

"Good morning, little one," she replies. Her dark

brown face wrinkles in greeting. "Where is Zirachi?"

"Visiting Mmesoma. But I can help you!" I take three big yams from the basket, her usual purchase, but she stops me.

"No, dear," she says. "Not so many today. Just one." Her thin fingers tremble as she takes a few cowrie shells from her bag.

"May the goddess bless you," I say quietly. I place a single yam on the mat and take the curved shells she offers in exchange.

"And you," she says, placing the yam in her bag, then walking away.

I look more closely at the people in the crowd. A hunched old man hobbles to another yam stall, where a hawkish vendor clangs a bell.

"Could you spare a yam?" the man asks in a meek tone, surely hoping his deference will earn him goodwill.

"Get away!" the vendor growls. "I can barely feed my own children." The old man ducks his head and shuffles on.

Zirachi comes back across the market square.

"What did Mmesoma say?" I ask.

"Much as I thought," she says with a sigh. "The poor harvest does not give her much to sell, but she does her best. The crowd is larger, but the buyers seem few." Her tone is even, but I can hear the worry in her voice.

A boy who looks close to my age and a small girl look longingly at the stalls of fragrant meats, warm flatbreads, and sweet plantain chips. The children are dirty and ragged, their cheeks angled and hollow. Whenever they draw near a stall, the vendor shoos them with cries of *Eh!* or *Go away!* The children scurry like mice and cling tighter to each other.

Ripe star apples sit bunched in the basket next to me. Zirachi's sharp eyes notice my sideways glance.

"Amara, we cannot help everyone who is hungry," she says.

"They don't need much. I'll give them the star apple I was saving for later."

"Then what will you eat? You're almost as thin as they are."

"I'm not that hungry." My stomach rumbles in disagreement. I pinch my lips and frown. "We give our harvest to the Eze," I say, "and he does not bring us rain or put food in our bowls. Why not to these?"

"Hush, child!" Zirachi chides. She shakes her head. "I see there is no reasoning with you." She bends down and puts two star apples into a cloth before tying it up. "Don't give it to them in plain sight," she says, "or we'll never hear the end of it from the other sellers."

I kiss Zirachi on the cheek, then run to the other side of the market with the little bundle.

Caught in the throng, I can't see the children, so I duck around a corner and wind through more stalls. Finally, I find them.

The children are not where fruits or vegetables are sold, but items of a different use. Magic.

The stalls are filled with earthy mushrooms, drying herbs, and objects so shriveled that it is impossible to know what they are. Zirachi and I sometimes come here to buy medicine, incense, or other items for our home.

At the edge of the market, an old woman leans over, giving the boy and girl some of her own meal. Dates and boiled groundnuts. Her wiry white hair frames a wrinkled, leathery face. The children gobble the food.

"I brought you more." I pull out the small bundle and hand it to the boy. He unwraps it and, seeing the fruit, gives the bigger star apple to the girl. They eat more slowly, licking every bit of juice from their cracked lips.

"Thank you," he says to me. The old woman

peers at the children with bright eyes, and he adds, "And thank you too, Auntie. This is the first we have eaten in days."

"My name is Amara. Where have you come from?" I ask.

"Benta," says the boy. "My name is Nweke." He wipes his mouth with the back of his dusty arm. "There's not much food among the people in the city, so my family left. We were separated during a dust storm, and I'm trying to find my uncle's family in the east."

The boy coughs, and I remove the water pouch hanging at my side and offer it to him. I can only imagine the hardship the children experienced to get here. The boy takes my pouch gratefully and drinks a large mouthful before handing it to the girl.

"I met Lebechi on the road," he says.

"Where's your family?" I ask her. She is younger than Nweke, and I guess not more than six years old.

"I don't know," she says, her voice soft and feathery. "I came from the mountains. My father said we must find food, and he told me to wait while he scouted the bush, but he didn't come back.

Lebechi wipes the dust from her eyes. "I went to look for him and met Nweke."

While the children speak, a few villagers listen

and whisper. People starving in the capital and in the hills. Why has the Eze done nothing? Have these children brought their bad luck to our village?

Nweke looks nervously at the crowd, and Lebechi clutches his hand. "We must go," he says. He hands the waterskin to me, but I shake my head.

"You may keep it."

"Thank you," he says. He bobs his curly head in gratitude.

"May Oala smile upon you, young ones." I've almost forgotten the old woman, so quiet she's been.

Pulling Lebechi by the hand, Nweke wiggles through the crowd, and soon they disappear.

The old woman's eyes fix on me. "I have a gift for you too, child."

"For me?"

The old woman hands me a dried yellow flower sprig.

"Yellow trumpet," she says, "for bravery."

"Thank you, Auntie," I say as I take the flower. A question sits in my mouth, but I swallow it and stick the blossom into my sash. "Goodbye!" Then I push back through the mass of people.

I don't see Nweke and Lebechi. The crowd has swallowed them whole.

I feel a strange prickling sensation. The children's tale has unnerved me, I tell myself. What if the Zare gnaws its way here to Danel? I pray that Zirachi and I never have to leave our home.

CHAPTER 3

THE PARCHED LAND

The low trumpet of a two-toned horn reverberates through the air. My heart sinks. Twice each day, the market boss strides in front of the temple and blows the twisted bush cow horn. The day's selling is over.

At our stall, I shake the sand from our mat and fold it. Zirachi and I stack our empty baskets. The cowrie shells in her money pouch rattle lightly, and I furrow my brow. We'll have the last of this year's yams for our evening meal, at least. I'd never say so, but I'd give anything for fresh pounded yams and a steaming bowl of rich pepper soup for dipping.

At our cart, Zirachi and I work in comfortable silence. I stroke Mango's rough mane, and the donkey nuzzles me with his soft nose.

"Ready to go home?" I ask him. Mango blinks his brown eyes placidly.

We rattle in the cart along the dusty road toward home, and Zirachi's gaze focuses on the path ahead. I cannot see her expression, only her stiff back and coiled bun tied with her orange scarf. The bright color makes it easier for our customers to find us, she says.

Over the creaking wheels, I listen for the signaling reverberations of the ikoro drum in the distance, our warning that a dust storm approaches. Weeks have passed since the last storm, but I am on edge with dread of the choking clouds of sand.

"Do you think a storm will come?" I say, looking at the horizon.

"No," Zirachi says, casting her eyes to the sky, "but I'm not a seer. Only the griots had that power. I do wish for rain, though. We're fortunate that the river runs so close to our farm and trees, but even it thirsts for more water."

At the market, opinions fly among the other sellers. When I went to the far side to bring food to the boy and girl, Nweke and Lebechi, I heard the mutterings.

"Chiku the potter says that Kun has been cursed."

"Amara," Zirachi says, glancing over her shoulder at me. She sighs. "You shouldn't repeat such tales."

"What other reason could there be?" I ask with a frown. "Do our prayers not reach the goddess? The elders collect our offerings at the temple, but the Zare only grows each day."

After a silence, Zirachi says, "Mmesoma thinks as you. That there is something broken in Kun. A crime that has not been atoned for." She clicks her tongue to urge Mango forward. "If the elders can't divine it, then the Eze must decide and act."

The Eze, our king, resides far away in Benta, the capital city. In my mind, he has done little for our village besides collect our taxes. "Maybe he doesn't know how bad it has become in Danel or other villages," I offer.

"That may be possible," Zirachi replies.

"Or maybe he knows, but he can't fix it."

"I hope to the goddess that is not true," she says. "Regardless, he will be here for the festival tomorrow. He will see."

I rub my thumb along the rough fibers of the baskets next to me. Zirachi glances back at me again.

"I sense there's more to your questions than the desert and dust storms."

For a moment, I say nothing and pull at some loose straws. Kun has many taboos. I touch my crescent birthmark, hesitating to speak of the taboo that matters most.

"Do you think I am the curse?" I ask at last.

My words hang in the air until Zirachi breaks free of her surprise. "No, Amara!" she exclaims. "You are my greatest blessing."

"But I'm an outcast, marked by the spirits. I have no ancestors, no past. Maybe—"

"You are my daughter. Finding you on my doorstep doesn't make you any less mine. I don't know what village gossip you're listening to, but you must ignore it. I will have words with whoever has put such ideas in your head." She looks down at me. "I wish I could tell you more. Who left you at my door . . . Who your ancestors are . . . I'm sorry that I don't know. I'm grateful to them, whatever their reasons were."

Our cart bumps along the gravelly road, and I listen to the steady clip-clop of Mango's hooves on the hard clay. I'm afraid I've upset Zirachi. She always speaks the truth, and I know it pains her that this time, the truth isn't enough.

Finally, she says, "Maybe someday you'll find the answers to your questions. But without the griots, those memories are gone. I'm afraid there's no more

17

of your story to learn, little one."

I lean my head against Zirachi's side, and she rests her hand on my shoulder. She is right, and I try to bury all my questions as the village of Danel shrinks in the distance.

At home, I carry the baskets to the small mud shed we use for storage, while Zirachi tends to Mango. We work in rhythm. When the baskets are stored out of the heat and Mango is curried and munching dry grass in his pen, we gather the remaining supplies.

"That's strange," I say. The front door is ajar, just enough to let us glimpse a glow from within.

Putting down her mats, Zirachi unsheathes a knife from her hip and presses against the hard clay wall of the house. Usually, she uses it to cut branches in the orchard or grass for weaving baskets. The way she holds it now is not so tame. She waves me back and places a finger against her lips.

Fear tingles down my spine as I crouch. Zirachi grasps the knife tightly and pushes open the door.

"Welcome," says a deep voice.

I peer around Zirachi. Embers from the hearth outline a shadowy form. As it leans toward the light, I raise my hand to stifle the scream that threatens to escape.

A horrible leopard head stares back, fangs bared. From its crown, long fronds of dead palm leaves hang, rustling as the creature moves.

Zirachi points the knife at the creature. "Who are you? Speak!"

The voice sounds amused.

"It is my home, too, though I barely recognize it," it says gruffly.

Realization dawns on Zirachi's face and she steps into the room.

"Okwu?"

The creature rises slowly, its fronds rattling like teeth. It raises its hands and removes what I see is a mask.

The same brown skin and amber eyes I know—and have seen so many times—now look at me from an unfamiliar face.

CHAPTER 4

OKWU

Zirachi's eyes narrow, seeming to pierce the darkness like the knife that trembles in her hand. "Okwu, is that you?" Her voice wavers across the empty space.

The truth of the question hangs in the air. No longer able to resist, I come from behind Zirachi. "It *is* you, isn't it?" I look between the man and Zirachi. The likeness between them leaves no doubt.

"Is this my greeting after being away so long?" he asks. "Sorry if I startled you. The mask ensured that no one would recognize me on my way here." The man walks forward, puts his hand on Zirachi's fist that's holding the knife, and lowers it.

The touch seems to unfreeze her.

"Okwu," she repeats.

"Yes, Zira," he says.

With an appraising look, he turns to me.

"And you, little girl. Are you my niece?"

His voice is even, like Zirachi's, but there is something hidden lying beneath it. Like a musician playing a false note.

"She is mine," she says through gritted teeth. "Amara, this is my brother," Zirachi says at last, the knife still tight in her grip.

Her eyes carry a flame of accusation that her words do not, and I can see that Okwu's words anger her. Zirachi has often said that Okwu must be dead. Why else would he have stayed away all these years, leaving her to care for the farm by herself?

"But what of you? I thought you dead."

Coughing sickness took Zirachi's parents years ago, then Okwu left to join the Nkume, the king's guard.

He turns toward the hearth, his eyes picking up the eerie light of the flames. "I was just a boy when our parents died," he says. "This house became a tomb and I had to escape. I don't regret leaving," he says, his voice steely. "I did what I must at the time." Softening his tone, he adds, "But I do regret not coming back for you."

"And you have lived all this time where? Doing

what?" Zirachi continues.

"I have been many places and seen much, but I want to hear of you and my niece, sister." Okwu turns toward us again, the light of the fire casting shadows across his face.

"Why were you in the village today?" I ask. As my fear drains, I remember the same leopard mask from the temple. This man may be Zirachi's brother, but there is something unsaid behind his words.

Zirachi looks between us in surprise. "What's this? You were in the market today and didn't speak to us?"

A furrow touches Okwu's brow for a moment, then is gone. "Yes," he says. "You have sharp eyes, little one. I saw you at the temple, Zirachi, but I didn't recognize the girl. I decided to come here and wait."

Okwu returns to his chair by the hearth and sits back. He looks around the room, and for a moment, I can see a shadow of the boy he must have been, but then it is gone. This new Okwu is nothing like the one in the stories I've been told.

Zirachi finally accepts what she hears and tucks her knife into her skirt. "Amara, go get our baskets. I'll put on some tea."

I scurry to obey. Zirachi stokes the embers in the hearth and puts a pot on the fire. She takes some kola nuts and dried star apples from our food baskets and prepares the table as she would for any guest.

"So, why did you return after all these years?" she asks at last, her back to her brother.

"I've come for the festival, and my conscience finally brought me to your door."

"So, you are not here to stay?" she says evenly.

"Stay!" he scoffs. "Of course not, Zira. I merely want to mend the walls between us before I must leave."

"Amara, get the tea," Zirachi says, as shrilly as the hissing pot on the fire. I look up in surprise. I've never heard her speak to me in such a way before.

Zirachi, sensing her rudeness, adds, "Please." I take the pot from the flames and carefully pour the steaming liquid into cups. Zirachi takes a platter of food along with the beverage over to Okwu, who accepts.

He sips the hot tea contemplatively, and Zirachi sits at the table next to me. After several awkward moments, I finally break the silence.

"I wish to know more about you," I say. "Won't you tell us?"

"For you, my niece, of course," he says. I notice Zirachi's scowl, but I lean forward to listen. "It wasn't easy in the beginning. After I left home, it took me many days' hard trek through the forest and valley to make it to Benta. I presented myself to the Nkume, and they laughed me away at first. 'We are Nkume, the Rock. You're too small and scrawny to be of use,' they taunted. 'Come back when you have some muscles on you.'

"But I stayed," Okwu continues. "At first, I waited by the gate when the members came in at dawn, and I was there again when they came out. Slowly, they became accustomed to me and saw me as a sort of errand boy. Soon I was in the castle and helping the leader of the Nkume with his armor and other tasks.

Okwu's eyes spark as he tells his tale. "Then one day they held a testing competition to see who was worthy to join. I had been practicing in the alleys and along the edges of the city since I arrived. Despite being a head shorter than the next smallest boy, I bested them all with my skill. They welcomed me into their fellowship, and I trained as a true member of the Nkume."

My eyes are wide listening to Okwu's story. I don't think I could best anyone by skill. I would be afraid to even pick up a stick, let alone a sword, if I were ever to fight someone.

"Well, it sounds as if you found a family of sorts, after all," Zirachi says, bitterness in her voice.

"I did," Okwu replies. "We are blood, Zira, but there can be more than that."

"What bonds are greater than blood?" she asks, her voice tight.

"Having a higher goal, a shared vision," he says simply.

"But aren't the Nkume only a lapdog for the court? Sent to do the Eze's bidding when loyalty must be demanded by sword rather than earned?"

My mouth drops to hear Zirachi speak so harshly. She has never spoken against the Eze in my presence. Clearly Okwu doesn't like her tone. He stands up.

"You would be wise to watch your words, Zirachi," he says, all traces of reconciliation gone from his voice and demeanor. His scowl is so twisted that even their family resemblance is dimmed.

"Knowing someone inside the Nkume can be a powerful benefit, but if you aren't careful, there may come a time that not even I can help you."

"What help have you been to me so far?" she asks. "'Onye aghala nwanne ya.' Do you remember those words, Brother? Our parents said that proverb often to remind us that we should look out for each other. 'Do not leave your brother or sister behind.'" Zirachi's chest rises and falls quickly. "You left, and I've been on my own to keep up our family farm for all these years. I see no benefit to you having joined the Nkume!"

Okwu's jaw is set, and he breathes slowly, like he's trying hard to keep his temper. "You have no idea how the world works, Zira." He glances at me with a strange look in his eye. "We all must make choices. Sometimes they are choices we later regret."

Okwu moves toward the front door as Zirachi and I watch, the leopard mask abandoned by the hearth. Opening the door, he turns and says, "I shouldn't have come. Some wounds can be too deep, but I thought . . ." His voice trails off as he looks out into the darkening sky. "I wanted to see how you were."

He lifts his cloak over his head, and again, he is cast into darkness and seems more shadow than man. "It's a dangerous world, Zira, and soon we'll all have to take sides," he says. "Make sure you can live with the choices you make."

With that, Okwu sweeps out of the door and into the open night.

CHAPTER 5

THE NEW YAM FESTIVAL

It is quiet after Okwu's visit. His appearance has poisoned the air and fear seeps into my skin. He had come to talk to Zirachi, but his eyes stayed fixed on me. Leopards are sure to be part of my dreams tonight.

I have wondered what became of Zirachi's brother, but I can see now that knowing the truth can be worse than knowing nothing at all. Okwu isn't the laughing brother Zirachi once described. That person never came home.

"I'm sorry," I say, finally daring to speak my mother's pain. "He was wrong to not send word for all these years."

At my voice, the stiff line of Zirachi's jaw softens. "He spoke one truth."

"What's that?"

"You can grow close to someone in ways that are stronger than blood." Zirachi gifts me a smile, though sadness dulls its light. "Tomorrow, we have much to celebrate."

We slice star apples and lay them by the fire to dry, a sticky sweet treat to take to the festival tomorrow. The day will be full of music and laughter, and, for once, everyone will have enough to eat. I try to put Okwu's visit out of my mind.

After we tidy the hut, Zirachi sends me to my sleeping mat. I watch her sitting by the fire alone, until I fall asleep.

In the morning, Zirachi gives me a gift wrapped in rough cloth. "Happy festival day, my love," she says warmly.

Not only does the New Yam Festival begin Kun's new harvest season, it also marks something more special to us. It's on this day that Zirachi found me all those years ago.

I unwrap the cloth and see one of Zirachi's akwete skirts and a matching halter, the one with indigo stripes that I've always loved.

"I think you've grown enough to fit this, no?" she says, holding it up to me. I beam as we both dress in our finest for the day.

Zirachi decorates my face with dots of white chalk in the traditional pattern of celebration and lets me do hers. When we're done, we get in the cart and ride to Danel.

In the village, the crowds are twice as large as they were yesterday. Word of the Eze's arrival has spread, and bustling throngs push us toward the temple.

Musicians line the streets, banging drums to the rhythm of our feet. I see Ifeoma, Mmesoma's daughter, standing near the courtyard with her mother, and we head over to them.

"A blessed festival day, Mmesoma," Zirachi says.

"And to you," she replies with a smile. "Ah, Amara! Look how you've grown. I remember Zirachi wearing this akwete." I beam and offer Ifeoma and her mother some of the dried star apple we brought.

"Ooh! My favorite!" Ifeoma says and pops a chewy piece into her mouth.

Dancers adorned in rich textured fabrics bob and weave in the courtyard to the rhythm of the drums. Next come the masquerades. Some on stilts, they all bear huge carved masks on their heads, visages of the spirits of the land. A pinprick tickles my neck as

I remember the leopard mask Okwu wore. As the masked dancers wheel in front of us, I move closer to Zirachi. Masquerades are connected to the gods and are both venerated and feared. Outsiders risk being cursed if they stray too close.

The horn sounds through the streets, and we turn toward the temple. A procession of armed men with red cloaks enters the courtyard, and Zirachi leans down and says, "The Nkume. The king is near."

The soldiers flank a raised platform where platters of roasted new yams rest. In a moment, a trumpet blasts, and I see the Eze.

King Udo is draped in robes of purple and gold. In his gloved hand, he carries a leather-handled horsetail, the traditional handpiece of royalty, and in his left, a wooden staff carved in the figure of a python.

"Why does the Eze wear only one glove?" I whisper to Zirachi. She hushes me and gestures for me to look at the ceremony.

The oldest person in the village usually speaks the blessing over the yams, but this year the honor goes to the Eze. He sits in the large chair that the elders have set out and extends his hands.

"People of Kun, as the old season ends, let us

embrace the gifts of the new. With the rising crescent moon, peace and prosperity shall come to the faithful. As it has been and always shall be, let us offer our gratitude to the goddess and partake in the first yam."

The Eze closes his eyes. "Oala, mother of earth and creation, thank you for your bounty. Accept this gift of thanks from your humble people and spare not your grace. Hold back the desert's teeth and send again your life-giving rain. We, your servants, give you praise."

"Amanye!" say the elders, and Zirachi and I repeat the traditional phrase of agreement with the crowd. "Amanye!"

"Now," says Eze Udo, "it is time to eat!"

Two servants offer a large platter of roasted yams to the king. He breaks off a piece of one and dips it in palm oil before consuming it.

"The new season has begun!" he shouts. The crowd claps, and voices and drumbeats rise. The Eze waves the platter away.

The people form a line to offer thanks to the Eze, and we join the queue.

"When I was a girl, I loved the festivals," Zirachi says to me with a smile. "We were never honored with the Eze's presence, but I remember the griots."

"Griots?" I ask. "Did they dance?"

"No." She laughs. "They did many things, but best of all, they told stories. Wondrous ones with bright colors that floated before our eyes and in our minds." She paused. "But I can't remember the stories anymore," she says with a frown.

"Neither can I," Mmesoma says. "Isn't that odd, Zirachi?"

"Yes," she replies. "Times were different then."

Ifeoma and I talk about what we want to eat first at the festival. Throughout the market, there will be tables with roasted yams, bean soup, fufu, and more deliciousness. Tomorrow might be porridge again, but today we can fill our bellies.

"Amara, stand straight and do what I do," Zirachi whispers. We're next in line. Mmesoma and Ifeoma bow before the Eze and offer him praise. He nods and waves the horsetail in acknowledgment. Next, Zirachi and I step forward.

"My king," Zirachi says, "blessings to you." She bows, and I follow her movements. When I look up, I notice the Eze's eyes move from my neck to my face. They are sharp and piercing.

"My child," he says. Then he nods and waves the horsetail again. Zirachi and I move to follow our friends. I glance back and see the king nodding to the next villager, but I can't help but feel the weight of his eyes as we leave the courtyard.

Away from the temple, it is not as joyous as it had been in the courtyard. Throngs of people crowd around where food is being distributed.

"There is enough!" one of the temple workers shouts, but his voice is drowned out by angry cries.

"My children are starving!"

"More, please!"

Soon, the crowd surges forward, and people run and begin snatching whatever they can.

"Zirachi!" I shout. The wave of bodies separates us, and I fall to the ground. Clouds of dust choke me, and I put my hands over my head to protect myself.

A horn blares, and heavy footsteps stomp closer. "Get back!" men shout. I catch a glimpse of red. The Nkume.

I feel hands pulling me up. "Amara, are you okay?" Zirachi asks, checking me over.

"Yes," I respond quickly. My legs wobble, but they hold. "I'm okay."

The market is in disarray. The hungry mob overturns tables and people grab whatever food they can. From the temple, I see more Nkume coming, and the Eze is nowhere in sight.

"We need to leave," Mmesoma says urgently. Ifeoma hugs her mother, and her eyes hold the same fear as mine.

Zirachi gives them a tight hug. "Go!" she says.

We all run as the village erupts in chaos.

CHAPTER 6

ARRIVAL OF THE THREE

The wind picks up as we ride home, and silt-brown clouds billow on the horizon. I cough on the grit and snuggle deeper among the empty sacks. Gray acacia trees overhang the dusty road, their seed pods rattling.

Zirachi and I have not spoken since we left the bedlam of Danel. She forced me into our cart and urged Mango as quickly as he would go.

Once the village shrinks from sight, she slackens our pace.

"I'm scared, Zirachi," I finally say. I'm not trembling anymore, but my heart still feels like a bird trying to escape a cage.

"I know, my love," she replies. "I would never have imagined—" she begins but stops. "But I should have. Times are hard and people are desperate. When we get home, we'll have some tea to calm ourselves, then pray."

"Do you think Mmesoma and Ifeoma are safe?"

"Oh, I'm sure they are. Their home is close to the square."

I begin to relax and close my eyes. The rhythmic rocking of the cart calms my body and my thoughts.

As the cart comes around a bend, it lurches to a stop.

"What's wrong?" I ask, raising myself from my comfortable nest.

Three figures in red stand in the road.

Zirachi slides her hand slowly behind her back to grasp her knife.

"Make way!" Zirachi calls out.

There is no movement from the men except the flap of their cloaks. Then the man in the middle says, "We've come for the girl."

Fear grips me, and I clutch Zirachi's sleeve.

"Who are you?" Zirachi asks, her voice steady, though I see her grip the knife more tightly.

"Give her to us, and you may live."

Zirachi whips the harness traces, and Mango charges forward. I tumble in the cart.

The man in the center lifts a wooden flute to his

mouth and plays. The strident notes wrap around my thoughts like a cord. I put my hands to my ears to block the sound, but I can't. He raises his chin toward Mango and blasts a barrage of notes. Our donkey brays loudly before collapsing, tipping the cart and throwing both Zirachi and me to the ground. I crawl over to Mango and stroke his rough coat as he convulses under the pain of some invisible force. He kicks his legs for a moment more, then goes still.

"No!" I scream. Zirachi's mouth tightens, and she pulls me to my feet. Cold metal is pressed into my hand.

Zirachi whispers quickly, "Keep it hidden. No matter what happens next, you run to the bush. Do not look back and do not stop."

"I won't leave you," I say, my fear growing.

"You have nowhere to go," the man calls. He carries no weapons, but I know danger lies in his hands and the sound of his flute. Cold sweat snakes down my neck. There is only one explanation for what has happened.

This man is a griot.

"Let the girl come forward. No harm will come to her," he says, his voice now laced with honey.

"I might have believed you before you killed my donkey," Zirachi spits. "You use Oala's power for evil. Why should I trust you?"

I peek at the other two men. Their hands rest on the hilts of curved swords, and they stand alert. Nkume. The king's guard.

Was this Okwu's business? Had he been sent to our village, not to reunite with his sister, but to spy? A foul taste rises in my mouth as I think of the betrayal.

After neither Zirachi nor I move, the griot says, "I tire. Give us the girl, or we'll take her. It makes no difference to me."

"You will take nothing!" Zirachi grabs a large branch lying by the edge of road and runs at the men. "Run!" she shouts at me.

I stand paralyzed. I want to obey, but fear roots me to the ground.

The griot lifts his instrument to his lips and plays, an undulating whistle that rises and falls. Zirachi stops in her tracks, frozen by unseen powers. He lifts his flute higher, and Zirachi rises above the ground. Stiff and shaking, she dangles with her arms out and head forced up. The branch she clutches falls to the dirt with a dull thud.

"We've been looking for you for a long time," the griot says, turning to me. "Come, and you won't be harmed. I'll even let this woman go."

I look helplessly at Zirachi, who still quivers in the air.

With a smile, he raises his flute toward me and plays. I wait for his conjury to pull me, bend me to his will as it had Zirachi. I wait, my fingers balled tightly in fear of what will come. The man's face twists, and he plays harder, faster. His fingers fly across the flute's wooden form.

My heart pounds, but nothing else moves except the dust that blows across the ground. I don't understand what is happening.

"Arghhh!" the griot growls. He shouts to the other men, "Take her!"

I look at Zirachi in panic and hear her croak one word, "Run!"

As the Nkume rush forward, I finally obey.

Blood thrums in my ears, and brown-red dust billows from my pounding feet. As I crash into the trees, my every step stabs like a betrayal. *How could you leave Zirachi?*

But there is nothing I can do. Zirachi doesn't want me to stay. With her last breath, she ordered me to flee. Staying would have wasted that sacrifice.

The griot who attacked us stays on the road. I can still see his anger and frustration as he blows into the flute and tries to make me obey. He can't.

I don't have time to wonder why. What worked on Mango and Zirachi fails with me. The two soldiers of the Nkume who flank him turn to chase me at the griot's order, and now they thunder behind me.

My lungs pump hot breath as I push myself headlong into the bush. A creeping presence raises the hairs on my neck, and I swerve. The soldier's stretching hand grasps only air.

The ground dips as I approach the river, and I slide down the steep slope. Far ahead, the bush drops off suddenly, and the river snakes below. I push myself faster as I dart around trees and duck under low branches. If I get closer to the cliff, I can run along the edge until I can double back toward the village for help.

I hear curses from the soldier behind me as he loses his footing and tangles with the underbrush. I dare a glance to my left and right, but the other soldier has disappeared.

Trees rush past and a branch whips me in the face. My eyes water with stinging pain, and in a blur of tears, I see too late the second soldier dashing toward me in a flash of red. His muscled arms open wide to grab me. Unable to stop my forward momentum, I fight. Fear and grief pour into my arms and legs. I will fight as hard as Zirachi did.

My foot strikes hard, knocking the soldier's hood back. Okwu's angry eyes glare back.

"How could you! You attack your own sister!"

I kick and flail as a scowling Okwu holds my arms tight. Branches snap and crack as the other soldier thunders clear of the brush, and Okwu's eyes dart toward the sound. The distraction is enough.

I swing Zirachi's knife up wildly. I catch Okwu's cheek, and he roars as the slit under his right eye turns bright red and blood spills down. The other Nkume is steps behind, but Okwu loses all reason in his fury. He wrenches the knife from my hand and drags me kicking and screaming to the edge of the bank. The Eke River churns muddy red on its way to the falls.

Okwu lifts me from the ground and dangles me over the edge. Instead of struggling to free myself, now I cling to his arms in terror as I look at the fast water below. The other soldier yells at him, but Okwu has no mercy in his eyes.

With a grunt, Okwu flings me into the waiting mouth of the snake.

I gasp. My rigid body reaches for Okwu as I fall away into nothingness. Then the Eke claims me.

I hit the water hard, and swirling brown surrounds me. Viselike pressure squeezes my lungs. There is no up or down, just the churning water that wraps itself around me like its python namesake. I struggle to free myself, but there is no escape from its powerful hold.

When my lungs feel like they will explode, I finally break the surface. My gasp for air is like a trumpet. Water swirls around me as the rapid current drags me downstream. I am far beyond the bank where Okwu threw me, and no one is onshore to help.

A distant roar makes my heart pound in panic. Stonefall. If I can't get out of the river, I have little chance of surviving the river's rocky cascade. A family in the village buried their son last summer after he slipped into the water and went over the edge. His broken body washed ashore a half day's walk from the bottom.

I grab frantically at anything that might help. Sticks and rocks jab and scratch me but offer nothing I can use as leverage.

A fallen tree jutting into the water gives me hope. I kick with all of my strength. When I am within arm's reach, I grab, but my fingers slide along the wet trunk. I gulp air and dig my fingernails in. The python will not let me go, and I am torn away by the current.

The rush of the water grows to a deafening thunder as I near the edge of the falls. The waning sun lights the water's rough surface, and the edge gleams like a knife. My mind freezes, and I can feel the snake's jaws about to close.

A memory of Zirachi floats before me. She is holding the clay python from the altar at home. "Oala protects us. Be willing to listen," she says. I don't know why I remember those words now, but they pull the panic from me like venom drawn from a sting.

I turn myself toward the churning falls, and instead of struggling, I wrap my arms around my chest. As I relax, the water feels different. Not the crushing snake, but the gentle rock of an embrace. At the edge, I kick, and the water foams around my free-falling form.

My arms and legs fly out once I hit the water, and panic threatens to fill me again. I stop moving and let myself float. The water responds. The Eke lifts me until the dim light of the sun appears. I kick with all my strength, and as I break through, sweet air fills my lungs.

My legs feel like jelly, but I kick anyway. Soon I am close to the shore. A fallen trunk stretches out its limbs, and I grasp it and hold tight. Hand over hand, I slide along the trunk until mud sucks under my feet. I let go and crawl out of the river. I have enough strength to pull myself to damp earth, then I drop, my head sinking into the soft red mud.

Footsteps pad closer, and fear prods me to run again. I can't. My body has nothing left to give.

CHAPTER 7

PIECES OF
THE TRUTH

A soft hand strokes my brow, and for a moment, I think I am back with Zirachi in our mud brick hut.

"Zirachi!" My eyes fly open, and I try to sit up, but wince in pain.

Terrible images flash through my memory. Zirachi trembling in the air, unable to move. A knife slash and blood dripping from Okwu's chin. The long fall into the gaping mouth of the Eke River.

"Rest, child," a voice says. "You need your strength."

I know that voice.

I turn to see white hair and a crinkled brown smile. It is the old woman from the marketplace.

I look around in panic. I don't know where I am. Dim shadows dance around mud brick walls. The room smells of earth and fresh herbs. A pot simmers on the hearth, filling the little room with warmth. My skin is covered in bruises and scrapes, and I ache all over.

"Where am I?" I ask.

"In my house," the woman replies, rising from her chair. "My name is Ebele. I found you by the river two nights ago."

"Two nights! Oh no!" I have to get back to Zirachi, and I struggle to get up from the cot. The old woman gently pushes me down until I rest on the soft blankets.

"You will not find her, small one," she says, shaking her head. "Your house is burned to ash. People in the village say no one survived."

I curl into a ball. When I ran, I didn't want to believe that I'd never see Zirachi again, but now the truth that I am alone in the world overwhelms me. Did the Nkume lock Zirachi in the house before they set it ablaze? I can't stop the sobs that shake me. Ebele strokes my hair but lets me cry until I have no more tears.

The old woman goes to the hearth and ladles steaming broth into a bowl. She urges me to take short sips. The warmth sinks into my bones, and it calms me.

I tell Ebele everything I remember. The three men in the road. Mango lying lifelessly in the dust. My throat tightens as I tell how Zirachi tried to protect me.

Ebele presses my hand. "You are safe now. My house is far from the village, and I have told no one that you are here." She gazes at me with a soft expression. "Oala has favored you."

"Favored? No, you must mean cursed. I have no family and no home."

"I did not say the favored do not suffer," Ebele says seriously. "Sometimes the good suffer *most*. Look at what has happened to our country," she says, gesturing toward her window. "The whole kingdom is suffering. The desert threatens to swallow us. But"—she wags a finger at me—"did not the mighty Eke bring you here to me? I do not believe that is chance."

I remember the vision of Zirachi holding the clay python. I shake my head.

"Much has gone wrong of late," Ebele says. She takes my bowl and hobbles over to the table. "Years have passed since the griots disappeared. Eze Udo rules, but the ground dies beneath our feet."

I frown. "But that man on the road must have been a griot."

Ebele shakes her head. "No true griot would do what you described. It is an abomination to Oala to take a life. A griot's powers are meant to bring life." She sits in her chair. "Of course. You are too young to remember the pastures and rains. Kun was bountiful."

"Do you believe the kingdom is cursed?"

Ebele stays silent a moment. "I am old, yet still I remember the way it was. The griots once advised the king, and their wisdom and magic kept balance. Without them, memory fades along with our land. Soon, there will be no one to remember Kun."

"Then it must be stopped," I say.

"Ah . . . it is not that simple," Ebele says, stroking the thin whiskers on her chin. "Who can help?"

"If one griot exists, there may be others. I could find them."

"I was right to give you that flower," Ebele says with a crooked grin. "There is strength in you. You survived enchantment and the river." The old woman grasps my hands in her wrinkled grip. "Maybe it is your fate to find them."

Fate. The word seems like a threat rather than a hope.

Night creeps through the windows; Ebele tucks

another blanket around me and blows out the candle.

"When did the griots disappear?" I ask.

"It should have been a night of great joy, but as it has again, it turned to sorrow. It was the night of the New Yam Festival. Twelve seasons ago."

I lower myself into the soft folds and stare at the fire. I never knew that.

The griots disappeared the same night I was found by Zirachi.

Ebele ventures to the village to buy supplies, and I am wrapped in worry while she is gone. The old woman chuckles when I confide my fears after she returns.

"Who would give heed to one like me? No one pays me mind, but my ears are sharp. And my eyes." She winks at me.

"What did you see?"

"More Nkume have come. They are searching house by house."

"For me?" My throat feels thick.

"They do not say."

"I must go." I hadn't considered the Eze's hand in the attack until now, but the Nkume are his guard. What have I done to anger a king?

"Tomorrow," Ebele says soothingly.

The next morning, I rise early. My fingers tremble

as I dress and put on the new clothes and warm cloak Ebele gives me. The old woman hobbles across the room and sets a large rough-sewn bag on the table.

"What is this?"

"Enough, I hope, to keep you safe on your journey," Ebele says.

In the bag, there is millet bread, nuts, dried fruit—enough food for several days—and a new waterskin. A glint catches my eye, and I pull out Zirachi's knife.

My voice catches. "Where—where did you find this?"

"It washed up by the water's edge. I thought you'd need protection. Does it look familiar to you?"

I blink back threatening tears. "It's Zirachi's." I slide my fingers along the smooth handle. I can almost feel her warmth in the wood.

"Oala brought it to us, then. She must want you to keep it."

I put the knife carefully back into the bag.

Ebele presses a small leather pouch into my hands. "These might prove useful as well."

I open the pouch. There is a piece of flint and firestone and a black candle. I also see a wooden ball and a small rock with a hole through the center.

"The candlewick is made from nightgrass from the riverbank. It will stay lit as long as the candle is in your hand," Ebele says. I touch the jet-black fibers at its tip.

"The ball is hewn of snakeroot," she continues, "and has been known to aid those on a journey. If you are lost, put it on the ground and ask for Oala's guidance. If she hears you, like the python, it will lead your steps."

I turn the rough little sphere in my fingers, then put it back into the pouch. I pick up the strange stone last.

"What's this?" I ask.

"That is an aggri stone," Ebele says, taking it from me. "Hold it to your eye, and it will reveal the truth of a place."

"The truth?"

"Just as people can be false, so can places. You cannot always trust your eyes."

Ebele puts the stone back in my hand. It is cool and smooth. I hold it to my eye. I see the same table and clay hearth. Same Ebele. I wonder if it is an ordinary stone, after all. I would give anything to have been warned that Okwu was not who he seemed—not a long-lost brother, but a heartless soldier.

I fasten the leather pouch to my waist and take out Zirachi's knife again. There is one more thing I must do before I leave.

As in all houses in the kingdom, Ebele's house has altars to her ancestors and to Oala. I walk to the altar for Oala and kneel. I have never done this alone.

"Oala, thank you for bringing me to safety. I ask for your protection again as I search for your servants, the griots." I hesitate, as the next words feel raw and new. I place the knife on the altar. "I honor my ancestor Zirachi, who is now with you in the underworld. May I have her strength and bravery."

I don't know how long I kneel, but finally I feel a warm hand on my shoulder, and it frees me to move again.

"Oala is goddess of justice and truth. I know she will guide you," Ebele says, her eyes bright.

"Thank you for your kindness." I hug the old woman and find that I don't want to let go.

"Safe journey, child. For all our sakes, as well as your own."

I pick up Zirachi's knife and place it in the bag of food and supplies. Tying the bag across my chest, I step over the threshold and set out into the forest. The trees tower above me, making me feel small. What would Zirachi think? I know. She would encourage me to find the answers.

I lift my chin and walk into the world.

CHAPTER 8

THE FOREST OF WHISPERS

After a long and winding trek through the bush, I reach the road. I crouch behind a twisted shrub and listen. Only my own heartbeat sounds in my ears. My village is back over the hills. In my mind, I picture the Eke River crawling along the edge of our farm. Past the burned husk that used to be our home. Smoke from the smoldering ashes must blow through our orchard and across the yam fields. Who will tend them now?

My eyes sting as I think of Mango. He liked how I used to comb his stiff fur until it was free of the sand and prickly burrs that bothered him.

Most of all, I think of Zirachi. I miss her strong embrace and calming voice. The way her tawny locs fell forward and she would tuck them behind her ear. Her smile when I learned a new skill or grew another inch taller.

We were all the other had.

I wipe the sweat from my forehead and take a breath. I have never been this far away from home. Where will I be at my journey's end? I swallow and summon my courage. Despite everything I have endured—drought and destruction, fire and famine—I am here. Alive. That is Zirachi's gift.

I walk on, but every snap or scuttle makes me drop and listen for soldiers. I feel like a soft-furred mouse trying to avoid the grain farmer's traps. I clutch the bag of supplies Ebele gave me and pick my path carefully, trying to stay hidden.

I don't exactly know what I am searching for. No one remembers where the griots live. Like everything else, memories of them fade like parchment in the sun. Ebele told me that magic is most powerful where there is calm water. Pools, ponds, or lakes. The desert devours these as it does everything else, but I take a chance on searching for the biggest, Lake Ugegbe. I check the slant of the trees to orient myself and move south toward the lower forests.

The landscape changes as I move farther away from Danel. The grasslands and shrubs begin to be replaced by patches of thick foliage. Above me, red-bellied monkeys skitter through the canopy. I creep below, wishing I could move as fast as they.

This far from Danel, I am more watchful of animals. I never worried about lions or jackals close to the farm, but in the open, I am no longer protected. I am grateful to Ebele for finding Zirachi's knife, but I pray I won't need its sharp blade.

The trees grow closer together, and eventually I find myself facing a path that would take me completely within their shade. But that does not feel like the right word. Under their branches is not the comforting gray of a normal canopy. The trees lean and stretch their crooked limbs, forming a tight gauntlet. A fist that might close around me. Nothing but shadow looks back.

I rummage in my bag and pull out the nightgrass candle. With shaking hands, I take my flint and stone and gather some dry grass. I will my hands steady as I strike the flint against the edge of the firestone. A flame sparks, and I put my candle near. As the little flame takes hold and glows, I grip the candle.

I step into the shadow and am swallowed by the forest.

Nothing exists outside of my candle's glow. I stretch my hand out to my side and can feel cold branches like bony fingers clawing at me. An unnatural breeze swirls around my feet, threatening to blow out my candle, but the nightgrass wick shines brightly and is not swayed by the air.

I think I hear voices, but I can't be sure. They are indistinct, like sighs in the wind.

Although I see no one, I feel watched. Farther into the forest, bright specks blink into view and then away. Unease pounds inside my chest.

My fingers slip along the sides of the hot candle, the soft black wax molding to my grip. My legs feel as if they are lead, and each step consumes a bit more courage.

Finally, a dot of light pricks the edge of the void. The end of the forest. A smile springs to my lips, though only the trees can see it, and I quicken my pace.

Despite the invasion of light from the forest's edge, the shadows do not diminish. Instead, they grow thicker and more oppressive. In my eagerness to get out, I stumble over a tree root. The candle drops from my fingers, and the forest goes black.

My heart thumps as I kneel and sweep my hands along the ground, desperate for the warm stump of wax.

"Sweet child," a lone voice rasps, "stay here with

us. We have not had a child for so long."

Sharp pebbles cut into my knees, but I ignore the pain. My fingers move frantically across the pitted road.

"Do not leave us," another voice persists, this one scratchy and hoarse. "No one remembers us. No one honors us. We are forgotten."

I suddenly understand who—or what—these voices are. They are ancestors that have been lost to memory. With the griots gone, fewer and fewer are left to keep their memory alive. My fear deepens. If they catch me, they won't ever let go.

"There is nothing for you outside the forest. No home. No past," the first voice whispers again, now joined by an unseen chorus. "Stay . . ." they wail.

"No!" I shout into the expanse.

"You cannot find the griots," a voice taunts. "None can find what does not wish to be found."

A cold chill sweeps past me. I strain to see anything, and I am scared to realize that I can.

Shadow against night. It moves toward me slowly, arms outstretched. As it gets closer, I can see it is small and childlike, but where its face should be, two pinpoints of misty light glow. The eyes remind me of every nightmare I've ever had.

Groping on the ground, my hand finally touches

something warm. The candle. I fumble in my bag for the flint and firestone. I have no tinder, so I use the hem of my skirt. I strike the stones hard against each other, and within moments a flame is born from the sparks. I quickly light the candle, then slap my hands over the burning skirt. My hand stings, but I don't drop the candle.

The shadow-child shrinks and hisses, and then it swirls into the canopy of the trees. "Stay with us . . ." the voices plead weakly.

I stand up, shaking but resolute. The breathy whispers become indistinct, and once more I can see light at the edge of the trees. Despite my throbbing hand, I pick up my bag and stride with my light out of the forest.

Once free, I don't stop. The scruffy patchwork of grass and trees continues, and I hasten to put distance between myself and the voices. I can still feel the glare of their pinprick eyes and the hiss of their breath in my ears.

With the forest behind me, my pulse eventually slows and my stomach grumbles. I stop beneath an outcrop of stone shaded by brush and take out some of the food Ebele packed for my journey. Whispers worm into my consciousness. At first, I think the spirits have followed me, but I soon realize these voices are human. I am not alone.

Have the Nkume found me? I crawl farther back into the bush and lie flat on the ground. My muscles tense, prepared to run—but a flicker of recognition makes me pause.

I peek from beneath the shadows. Nweke and Lebechi, the boy and young girl I met in the market, walk mere steps from my hiding place. I can't believe my eyes!

"Nweke?" I say, crawling out of the leaves.

The boy jumps in fear and then his face relaxes in recognition.

"It's you!" Lebechi says, scooting forward through the leaves and grabbing my hand.

"Where did you come from?" I ask, my heartbeat slowing in relief.

"After we left the village, we followed the river," Nweke says. "My uncle's village is east, so we walked until we saw the forest. I've heard stories about that place, so we stayed close to the water's edge until we passed it."

"That was wise. The forest truly is haunted. I almost didn't escape," I say.

"How did you make it through?" Nweke asks.

I take out the nightgrass candle that Ebele gave me and explain how it repelled the spirits and allowed me to break free from the forest.

Nweke's and Lebechi's eyes widen as they listen.

"Oala must have led me to this spot knowing I would find you. I'm so glad to see you again," I say.

"Where are you going now, Amara?" Lebechi asks. "Will you come with us?"

"I can't," I say. "I'm looking for the griots."

"Griots?" Nweke asks in surprise.

"Yes. You should come with me! If we find them, the griots can help you locate your uncle's family, Nweke. I'm sure of it!"

Nweke looks thoughtful, but Lebechi doesn't hesitate. "Oh yes! We should go with you. I would love to meet a griot!"

"Well, I don't know if I can find them."

"Then we will help you," Nweke says. "It's the least we can do to repay your kindness. Maybe you're right. I've been searching for my family for weeks. If there are still griots, perhaps they can help."

"I'm sure they exist—at least . . . the bad ones do." My throat feels tight, but I manage to tell them about Zirachi and the attack on the road.

"How do we know they're not all bad?" Lebechi whispers, as if saying the words might cause griots to appear.

I shake my head. "No, Oala would not have sent

60

me on this journey only to find evil. Zirachi always said that where there is bad, there is good. Sometimes it only needs someone to look for it." I cup Lebechi's round cheeks with my hands and smile.

"Are you hungry?" Nweke asks. "We gathered some groundnuts yesterday." They sit with me, and I take the nuts gratefully. I share the dried star apples and other food from the sack Ebele gave me.

When we finish eating, I stand and pick up my bag. "Come," I say. "We're losing the light and should keep moving."

Lebechi takes my fingers in hers, and Nweke walks ahead of us. I hold the little girl's hand as we continue our trek east.

CHAPTER 9

A TANGLED PATH

The sun starts to descend in the sky, and we know we must find shelter for the night.

"Look," Nweke says, pointing ahead.

At the far edge of the grassy plain, a thick patch of bush extends in both directions. It looms above our heads once we are near.

"I can't see a way around it," I say. The thorny scrub grows so close that it hides what lies beyond. We walk along the living wall until I finally see a narrow opening into the bush.

"Wait," I say. I peer through the dimming light and see that the path branches at the end. A maze?

"We'll need to go through," I say, but Nweke looks unsure.

"How do we know what's inside?"

"What choice do we have?" I reply. "We need to find shelter before night, and the bush stretches beyond the eye in both directions. Staying here in the open would make it too easy for the Nkume to find me."

Nweke sighs and nods. We both hope it's the safest path, but we can't stay where we are.

"Come, Lebechi," I say. "Stay close to me."

I step into the bush maze. I walk slowly, letting my vision adjust to the gray light. The back of my hand brushes against the bramble, and I cry out in pain. An angry red line throbs on my skin.

Lebechi screams as the same happens to her. "Amara, it hurts," she whimpers.

Nweke turns to go back, but he can't. Silently, the maze has closed around us, and a wall of thorns stands in our way. He tries to use his bush knife, but it won't cut through. He ends up gasping in pain instead, as fiery streaks mark his hand.

I hold my arm to my chest.

"Stay away from the bush," I say through gritted teeth. "We must keep going, but carefully so we don't risk touching it again."

We move into a line, me in the front and Nweke bringing up the rear. Stepping forward more cautiously, I squint to see the edges of the maze, and the thorns prick me as my shoulder grazes the other side. How far have we gone? Guilt grips my heart. We could be trapped, and I led the others into this danger.

I remember the little ball Ebele gave me and I signal to the others to stop. Digging into my bag, I pull out both the snakeroot and the nightgrass. I give Nweke the candle while I strike the flint to create a spark. After we light the candle, our hands shaking all the while, I take it back and hold it up.

Bush surrounds us on all sides. It trembles and shifts, tightening its circle of thorns. We huddle closer together, and our breath comes fast. I wonder if there is any escape.

I hold the ball tight and whisper, "Oala, guide us!"

I set the snakeroot in front of us and pray that the goddess has heard. The snakeroot doesn't move, but the thorns do. The circle closes, and I wait for the piercing pain that will come next.

Then the root rocks. I clench my hands together and say, "Oala, please guide my steps!" The ball rocks again and rolls. It stops at the foot of a thorn bush. There is no way ahead.

Without warning, the bramble shudders and pulls

itself apart, like an invisible machete has cleaved it from top to bottom. Even its twisted roots pull back from the ground to open a path.

When the bush moves, the snakeroot rolls onward. We inch after it, and my pulse pounds as the bush closes behind us, nipping at Nweke's heels.

It stops again. There is path before us, but the ball rocks to the right. The bush shudders and then clears a new path. The snakeroot rolls to the side, and we follow. I grasp the nightgrass candle tightly and watch the rough wooden sphere rolling before me.

After more twists and turns, it stops. The bush makes one last great shudder and then peels back to reveal a forest. I grab Lebechi's hand and hurry through, with Nweke close behind. I snatch up the ball, and as soon as Nweke is out of the maze, the thorns crash shut like a dog's snapping jaws.

We all drop to the ground where we are, too frightened to move.

The sun dips through the clouds as we trudge through hilly woods. I have never walked so far, and every part of me aches. The vanishing sun takes its warmth over the horizon.

"I'm cold," Lebechi says. I wrap my arms around

her to stave away the creeping chill as we look for a safe spot to rest.

We come to a cleft of rocks and find the opening to a small cave, not big enough to stand in, but large enough for the three of us. I worry about what might be lurking in the places I can't see, so we don't go too far back into its mouth. Nweke and I gather dried leaves to make warm nests for each of us.

"Try not to rub your arm," he says to Lebechi gently.

"But it still stings . . ." she fusses, scrunching her nose.

"I know," I say. "At least we're safe now. Give it time, and the pain will subside." She nods and lies down in the little nest that I helped her make.

"We would never have made it through without you, Amara," Nweke says. "You thanked Oala for bringing us to you, but I think it should be the other way. I must thank her for bringing you to us." He smiles shyly, then says, "Good night."

Curled up in the pile of leaves, without a roof over my head or an altar I thank Oala again. For leading us through the maze and to this shelter. And for finding friends for me along the way.

Tears wet my cheeks as I think about Zirachi and

how much I miss her. She would be proud of me for making this journey.

As I drift into sleep, I imagine her voice. "You are brave enough."

CHAPTER 10

THE REMNANT

Morning light filters through the canopy as we scatter the leaves of our makeshift beds.

We skirt along the edges of trees, to stay hidden. In the distance, we catch glimpses of the mountains.

The countryside changes as we move farther along. Wisps of green poke through the brown foliage. Nweke crouches and places his hand on the forest floor.

"There is water," he says.

Soon the trees thin and shards of light penetrate from above. We step out onto the edge of a vast, shining lake. Only the lapping of water on the shore interrupts the quiet.

"It's beautiful," Lebechi says.

This must be Lake Ugegbe. Again, I'm thankful

for Ebele's wise guidance. The lake nourishes the area much as the river does the area near my home. Still, I can see where the water has withdrawn from the banks, leaving caked and dried mud behind.

Something tells me there is more beyond what we can see and hear. A feeling in the air. Yet even in this place of hidden mysteries, Kun grows weak.

"Ebele said that if the griots still exist, they may be here," I say.

"I don't see anything," Nweke says.

It's true. I scan the placid water, but it reveals nothing.

Then I remember the aggri stone. Ebele said it could reveal the truth of a place. I open my bag and pull out the small gray stone. I look around again, not seeing anything unusual, and wonder what truth the stone might see.

I close one eye and lift the aggri stone to the other. "Oh!" I gasp.

"What is it?" Lebechi asks.

"It's a temple!" I say.

In the middle of the lake stands an immense building. I take the stone away from my eye and look again: there is nothing. Putting the smooth stone against my eye once more, I see the gray temple far out in the lake, waiting for us—for me.

I give the aggri stone to Nweke, who looks through the opening. "I see it too!" he exclaims. "This is truly a wondrous place."

I walk to the edge of the water. I know where to go but not how to get there. I'm not a strong swimmer, and after my time in the river, I have no desire to enter the water again. A feeling tells me that it would take more than a simple swim to make it to that island.

I think again about Ebele's words. *Oala is goddess of justice and truth.* I face toward where I saw the temple through the stone and think. Zirachi once said the goddess despised all injustice and falsehood. Perhaps to find the griots, I must vow the same. I call out in a strong voice, "I seek the truth!"

"Look!" Lebechi shouts.

A rushing sound rises from the water, and a slab of rock emerges near the shore. The flat surface is slippery with mud, but wide enough for a person to stand on. Is this the way across? I carefully step onto it. Before I can decide what to do next, another stone pushes up from the murky waters.

"Come!" I say to my friends. "We go this way."

"What if I fall?" Lebechi says. "I can't swim."

"I'll help you," Nweke says, grasping her hand firmly in his and then leading her to step on the stone.

I step forward, and Nweke and Lebechi follow. When their feet leave the previous stone, it instantly disappears into the lake.

"We'll drown!" Lebechi cries.

"No. I won't let that happen," I say. "See? Our next step is before us." And it is. The stone behind us is gone, but in front of us a new one rises. The three of us soon find ourselves hopping along a fleeting path across the water, each stone sinking as we move to the next.

When we reach its center, the lake swallows another stone, but a new one does not appear. We stand shakily on the final stone with nowhere to go. I wonder if Lebechi might be right and that the water may claim us after all. A wave of panic rises in my throat.

But as before, I sense that there is something here. I reach out and feel a quiver in the air, as if the lake is holding its breath.

I haven't come this far to give up. I step onto the open water.

"No!" Lebechi and Nweke yell.

Instead of plummeting into the lake's cold grasp, my feet crunch on the rough gravel of the shore. I am on the island, and a fortress of rock looms above me.

I turn around and see Nweke's and Lebechi's terrified expressions. They can't see me! To them, I have simply vanished. I hope they can hear.

"I made it!" I call. "Trust me! Step forward, and you'll be safe."

Instead of reassuring them, my bodiless voice frightens them more, especially Lebechi, who wraps her arms around Nweke and tucks her head under his arm.

"Nweke, I'm still here. Follow my voice."

"Okay," he says weakly.

Nweke holds Lebechi's hand and whispers in her ear. They linger at the edge of the stone, then step forward.

"I've got you!" I cry as my friends' feet crunch on the stony shore. I grab them, and the two look around in amazement.

"Come," I say. I follow a path to my right that curves around the building until we come to a huge door. I raise my fist to knock, but the door swings wide before I touch it. I see no one, but clearly we are being invited in.

We walk through the open door.

Inside, we find ourselves in a vast hall. Footsteps pad toward us, and I whirl around. A young man wearing a plain tunic approaches.

"Welcome, Seekers of Truth," he says. "Come with me."

"Who are you?" I ask.

"My name is Mataye," says the young man. "I'm an apprentice."

"To the griots?"

Mataye nods. "Please, come with me."

In stunned silence, we walk behind the young man, our eyes absorbing all. Huge arches decorate the hall, and narrow windows cast stark shadows across the stones.

"You're learning magic?" Nweke asks.

Mataye looks at him with a slight smile. "Some. I help Griot Uchendu with his work."

Questions race through my mind. "Who is Griot Uchendu?"

Mataye does not answer. We follow him down a narrow hallway. Along the way, we pass other men and women dressed as Mataye, busy with their tasks. I wonder if they are apprentices too. Finally, we enter a large room with a massive wooden table. Two people sit in conversation, but look up as we approach.

"Teacher," says Mataye, "here are the children."

"Thank you," the man says. Mataye nods and leaves the room.

"Welcome, children," the old man says. He has a wiry beard that is a tangle of gray whiskers. His brown eyes are kind, but shrewd.

"Please, sit." He beckons to empty stools. I walk forward awkwardly and sit, and Nweke and Lebechi do the same. "I am Uchendu. This is my daughter Griot Ndidi."

The woman is about Zirachi's age and wears robes similar to Uchendu's. Her skin is the color of a kola nut, and her hair is sectioned and twisted into several tight knots ornamented with coral beads.

"We've been waiting for you for a long time," she says, looking at me warmly. "It's a blessing from Oala that you are here." I notice her glance at the crescent birthmark on my neck.

"How could you know I would come?"

"Your arrival was foretold," says Griot Uchendu.

Nweke and Lebechi glance at each other but stay silent.

"I have so much to ask," I stammer. The questions in my head make me dizzy.

"The answers may not be what you expect, Amara," the old man says. "First, tell me, why have you come?"

I swallow hard. "The land is dying, and people are starving across the kingdom." I turn to my friends. "This is Nweke and Lebechi. I met them in Danel. They've lost their homes and families." I pause. "Then the Nkume came. And a man with a flute.

My family—Zirachi and I—we were attacked . . ." Tears sting my eyes, but I wipe them away and continue talking.

Griot Uchendu rests his fingertips together while he listens. When I finish, he grips the arm of his chair and stands, leaning on his carved wooden staff. As he limps toward the hearth, I wonder if I've said something wrong and look at Nweke. He seems as confused as me, though.

At last, Griot Uchendu speaks, his voice somber. "I'm sorry for your pain, child. For all your pain," he says, turning back to look at us. "The trouble in our kingdom grew long before you all were born. We are only now seeing its rotten fruit." He sighs, and Griot Ndidi bows her head.

"Many years ago, a rift formed within our kingdom, and a group of griots turned from our teachings and attacked their comrades," he says. "Many brave griots were killed in the battle. So much knowledge was lost." Uchendu shakes his head sorrowfully. "We in this fortress are all who remain. The remnant."

"Those who turned we call the Ugha," Griot Ndidi says. "The false ones." She looks at Uchendu, and a sense of agreement seems to pass between them. She continues, "What you say of their deeds proves to us that they have chosen a twisted and evil path.

I'm sorry for what's happened to you."

"Why would they attack me and Zirachi?" I say.

The griots don't answer, but instead, Uchendu asks another question: "What do you know about our last king?"

"Eze Udo?"

"No. The king before him, Eze Ikemba."

I scrunch my nose. Ikemba? I don't know that name.

"Eze Ikemba," Uchendu says, "was our last king, but when he died a regent was named to rule until a new king or queen could be determined."

"What does that mean?" I ask.

"Oala's wisdom guides us. We are her people, and our leaders are born of her from the earth. When a ruler dies, Oala sends her heir." Griot Uchendu pauses. "Udo, the man who now calls himself king, is a thief who has stolen the throne."

Eze Udo is not our real king? I look at Nweke and see the same disbelief and shock that I feel. How can this be?

"Why doesn't Oala help us?" I say at last. Such lies and treachery would be an abomination to her.

"She has," Griot Ndidi says. "Ikemba has an heir. Oala's child has been born."

CHAPTER 11

CHILD OF THE EARTH

"Oala's child? I don't understand," I say.

Griot Uchendu closes his eyes, and weariness etches his countenance. "Of course you don't," he says. "Memory has faded since we griots were driven into hiding and have become separated from the people. There are so few of us left."

"Please. Tell us," Nweke says.

Griot Ndidi walks to Uchendu and places her hand on his arm. "Tell them, Father," she says quietly.

"It has been too long since I have done the work," he replies.

"But it is time," Ndidi says.

Uchendu leans on his staff and walks to a table that contains several musical instruments. I've seen such before on festival days when musicians play songs to celebrate the harvest. A five-stringed lute with leather stretched over its boat-shaped form. A balafon with its resonant wooden bars resting on a bamboo frame. Several drums, including a polished log-shaped ekwe and a metal pot drum.

Griot Uchendu stops and picks up a long-necked instrument I don't recognize. "Ah, my old friend," he says, caressing the worn handle, "help me tell the tale." He returns to us and sits, placing the large calabash base between his legs and positioning his fingers along each side of its many strings. "This is a kora, the main instrument of the griots," he says. He strums lightly, and Nweke, Lebechi, and I look at one another. Not only can I hear the sound, but I can also *feel* the vibration of the strings. It reminds me of the flute notes that tightened around me before, but this music is warm and inviting.

Ndidi picks up an instrument that looks similar to Uchendu's but it is smaller. When she returns to her seat, I notice that she holds it so that the strings are directed away from her, unlike the kora. Her fingers strum out a rhythm that wraps around the one Uchendu plays. The song grows more resonant.

"Hear now as I tell the story of Kun!" Uchendu's voice is rich and sonorous as he begins to speak.

I've never heard a griot tell a story. Zirachi sometimes told animal tales at bedtime to help me sleep,
but this is different. Energy quivers in Uchendu's
words, like the power I felt when the other griot,
the Ugha, attacked us on the road. This is stronger.

"Long ago, when people first walked the world,
it was bare and nothing grew. They cried out to the
earth to help them. Oala answered." As Uchendu
speaks, his fingers remember the story and fly across
the strings of the kora. His words float in the air and
a picture forms. I can *see* the story! Griot Ndidi's
voice accompanies him, a low and melodic hum.

"A great light like a thousand suns exploded from
the ground, and when it dimmed, there was a child.
The people took it into their village. Wherever the
child went, the earth bloomed. Green burst from
the ground, cool water rose from springs, trees bore
sweet fruit. As the child grew, he showed wisdom
and bravery, and when he reached adulthood, the
people made him their king." The griot's words
paint a lush scene of this first king. Above us, I see
him laughing, growing, caring for the people and
the realm.

Uchendu's voice drops.

"The king grew old. He remembered from where
he had come and foretold that another would come

to take his place. Before he died, the king named one to care for Kun until Oala birthed another ruler. In time, she did.

"As with the first, a blinding light came from the earth, and when it was gone, an infant lay wrapped in grass. A girl! She was taken to the palace and raised as a queen. The regent watched over the kingdom until she was of age. The royal line continued in this way for over a thousand years—born of magic—our prosperity bound with the earth."

The words and music float in the air and wrap around us. My mind spins. The griots' story fills some emptiness in my head, and now I feel the tale has always been there. I have *always* known this history. Haven't I?

But I want more.

"What went wrong?" I ask. Nweke and Lebechi echo my question.

Griot Uchendu's fingers fly across the kora, and we fall silent. The strings vibrate and spin a plaintive melody as he continues his song. Ndidi's echoing chorus is subdued. The scene in the air shifts.

"Whenever the king or queen does not live to the day of the arrival of the new earth child, the land feels the loss. Drought and famine rear their heads.

Never for long, but enough to remind the people of Oala's blessings. Oala rules life and creation, but also the underworld and death. Her children wield all the might and terribleness of the earth, so a new king or queen must learn to control their power.

"Some in Kun were gifted with special talents and abilities. They served as protectors and were tasked with guiding the earth child in knowledge and wisdom. These were the first griots."

Uchendu plays the final notes of his song as Ndidi plucks the strings of her instrument in harmony. When finished, Uchendu rests his hands on the kora's base. The notes and images linger in the air for a moment then fade. Weariness lines the griot's face. "Such is the history of Kun. Remember it well, children. It must not be forgotten."

Questions spark like fireflies in my mind.

"How is Eze Udo a thief?" I ask. "You didn't explain."

Uchendu drops into his chair with a groan. "Our good Ikemba lived an extraordinarily long life but he died before the heir arrived."

"So Udo is not Oala's child?" Nweke asks.

"No. Eze Ikemba and his queen fostered a young boy—Udo. His name, ironically, means 'peace,'"

Griot Ndidi says. "The king loved him well and meant for the boy to become regent when he grew to a young man."

A frown lines Griot Uchendu's brow. "But Udo grew to love power. The signs were clear that the arrival of Oala's child was imminent, and Ikemba began to fear what Udo might do." Uchendu shakes his head. "I should have sensed it too . . . But I was ignorant to problems in my own house," he says, his voice thick with regret. "My last apprentice, Nduka, wanted to learn conjuring that I would not teach. In spite, he took his voice and sacred knowledge to Udo and betrayed the griots. Udo offered influence and power, and other apprentices joined him."

"And what of Eze Ikemba?" I ask.

"He died," Ndidi says.

"More from a broken heart than anything else," says Uchendu. "And the queen soon after. Udo was left in control and did something terrible."

A cold tingle raises the hairs on my neck. Lebechi clasps Nweke's hand.

"Udo's griots used their knowledge of sacred ways to unravel the time of the child's coming. Arriving before us, with murder in his heart, he performed an evil spell. He tried to take the infant's power so he would have Oala's gifts, but it did not work. The goddess protected her heir. In anger, Udo intended to kill the babe."

My hand flies to my mouth.

"He did not succeed," Griot Ndidi says reassuringly, "but the Ugha's song weakened Oala's protection. Magic could not kill the child, but now a sword could."

The story grows more horrible, and I can barely listen. Who would be evil enough to kill a baby?

"A fight ensued, and during the skirmish, a young member of the Nkume was sent after the child. But Udo did not know the heart of this man. Instead of doing the terrible deed with which he had been tasked, the soldier brought the child to us," Ndidi says.

Nweke and I look at each other in surprise.

"We sang a song of memory to the guard," Griot Uchendu says, "so that the Ugha would not learn the truth. He returned to them with blood on his sword and the memory of killing the child."

"What happened to the baby?" Nweke asks.

"The child was not safe with us. Too many had been killed or had defected to Udo's side, and we who remained were being hunted by the Nkume," he says with a sigh. "It was decided that I would take the child to a safe place. No other griots would know where that was. I journeyed long and far, with the infant tucked under my cloak. In a tower long abandoned, I sealed her inside with a song of protection. She has remained hidden all this time. Waiting."

"Waiting for what?" I say.

"For you," Uchendu replies. "Your destinies are tied together. Together you have grown, and together you will help bring life back to our home."

"I have no magic," I say, my voice soft.

"That's not true. You escaped the Nkume and the Ugha," Ndidi says with a smile.

I remember the other griot's angry glower as he tried to do to me what he had done to Zirachi.

"The tower has been her haven," Uchendu continues, "but it has also been her prison. You must go to her."

My mind is too exhausted to focus any longer, and Ndidi notices. "Father," she says to Uchendu, "the children are tired. They have journeyed long to reach us."

"Yes, of course," says Uchendu. "Even learned people have difficulty comprehending the complexities of such matters. You all must rest."

Ndidi takes the kora from Uchendu and returns both instruments to their tables. Griot Uchendu holds his hand out toward us. We gather near him and he clasps my hands between his. They are warm and firm.

"Mataye," he calls. The young man returns and bows to the griots. "Please take Amara and her friends to their rooms. Bring them food and drink."

"Yes, Teacher. Please come," Mataye says to us.

We follow him out to the hall and Mataye shuts the enormous wooden doors behind us. Before they close, I see Uchendu rest his head in his hands.

CHAPTER 12

THE JOURNEY BEYOND

I lie on the soft cushions of the bed and drift into sleep. I am standing in a torchlit tunnel with walls made of stone. Behind me, shouts ring and swords clash. The sounds of battle. I walk until I come to a door. It is immense, five times the height of any I have ever seen, and barricaded with an enormous wooden plank.

A shadow moves behind it, and I lie on the smooth coldness of the floor to look underneath. Small feet stand on the hard clay.

I rise and look at the door again. This time it is not immense, but normal size. I puzzle at this. I put my hands around the board that fastens the door and try to lift it, but it won't move. No matter how hard I pull, it will not budge.

The clang of swords and the angry voices are louder and coming toward me. Fear takes root, and I bang on the door.

"Let me in!" I shout.

Silence.

I bang again. The sharp cries are closer.

A voice from the other side of the door, barely audible against the fray, calls, "Let me out!"

"I can't," I shout. "Please, let me in!"

The world shifts. Rather than coming from behind me, the battle sounds are now on the other side of the door.

The door shivers with intense banging. The voice, now laced with panic, repeats, "Find me, Amara!"

I jump back, staring at the door and hearing the thuds like a drum in my head.

"Help!" says the voice before it is drowned out by the pounding.

I open my eyes, but the thundering noise doesn't stop. I sit up. The booms of an ikoro echo outside, and I run to the window to confirm my fear. It is barely evening, but the sun has been erased. A wall of dust boils in the sky. It rushes in galloping billows across the horizon, devouring all in its path.

My door slams open. Mataye holds an oil lamp high and shouts, "The storm is almost here!" Nweke and Lebechi tremble behind him.

I run to the door, and Mataye grabs my hand and pulls me down the hall.

"Where are we going?"

Mataye does not answer. We run until we come to a large ornate door. Mataye shoves it open without a knock. "Teacher, I have them. You must come!"

"I have him!" Griot Ndidi waves us on as she helps Uchendu to the door.

"I have not lost my ability to walk yet," Uchendu says with exasperation.

"Yes, but we must hurry," Mataye says. "Everyone else is below. The storm is upon us." As he speaks, the air fills with a whistling cry. Choking sand whips through the outer windows.

We shield our faces as we stumble toward the stairs. Mataye's lamp has blown out, so we use our hands to guide us as we descend into the bowels of the temple.

At the bottom of the stairs, Mataye relights his lamp from one of the flickering wall torches. We all enter the first storeroom.

"I must check on the others," Ndidi says once we are safe, and she runs down the corridor. Mataye shuts the door firmly when she is gone. The howls of the wind dull, but the walls shudder as the storm rages. The air is thick with dust, and Mataye gives us damp cloths to tie around our noses and mouths to make it easier to breathe.

I remember doing this with Zirachi. We didn't have anyplace to run in our hut, so we huddled under blankets and waited for the winds to die down and the dust to stop falling.

The storms have become worse, and this one lasts longer than any I remember. I sit close to Nweke and let Lebechi lay her head in my lap. Uchendu covers us with his cloak.

Later, I peek from beneath it and watch the old griot and Mataye in quiet conversation. I think of the story Uchendu sang, and the bright images dance again in my mind.

The world is falling to dust, and the only one who can stop Kun from dying is Oala's child.

The next morning, a soft hand on my shoulder awakens me. "Sorry, but Griot Uchendu would like to see you," Mataye says.

The storm has abated, and soft candlelight warms the storeroom where we shelter. Lebechi still snuggles against me.

"Wake up, little bird," I say to her. The girl stirs and opens her eyes.

"Oh, I had the most awful dream," she says. "A monster was trying to eat us."

"That's not far from the truth," Nweke says as he stretches. "The Zare spreads and may eat us yet."

"Don't say that," Lebechi says with a shiver.

"Nweke, don't frighten her," I chide. Looking at Lebechi, I say, "We're safe here."

"I didn't mean it," he says to Lebechi. "Amara's right. We're safe."

"Come eat," Mataye says to us. He puts a tray on the small table that sits nearby. There are roasted yams, fruit, and dried meat. I pick up a star apple. It looks almost as inviting as the ones we grow at home, but I'm sure it won't taste as sweet.

"Thank you."

"When you're done, I'll take you to Griot Uchendu." Turning to Nweke and Lebechi, he says, "I also am in need of help from the two of you, if you're willing."

"Yes, of course!" Nweke says.

Mataye smiles and leaves.

I chew steadily on the food. Lebechi's dream

reminds me of my own dream about the locked door. I have never dreamed that clearly. The sharp clash of swords and the thump of my fist on wood still echoes. Both Uchendu and Ndidi say my destiny is linked to Oala's child, but I don't understand how.

We finish our meal and walk to the doorway to look for Mataye. He waits down the hall. "We're ready," I say.

He brings me to the large hall before taking Nweke and Lebechi with him to another part of the temple. Several griots talk with Griot Uchendu, who is standing next to a narrow window that looks across the lake. He turns when I enter.

"Come, child," he says. "We have much to discuss about your journey."

"There's not much more to tell," I say.

"No, I mean the journey you take next. Your task is to free Oala's child and bring her here."

My eyes widen. "I—I can't do that."

He studies me. "It is your choice. I cannot force you, but know that you are the only one who can free her. I will give you what help I can."

I take a slow breath. Zirachi says we must think of others before ourselves. Here is another person who needs my help, like Lebechi and Nweke. Someone who could make the kingdom right again.

"Yes, I'll go," I say at last, "but I'm not sure I'm ready."

Griot Uchendu nods. "I believe you are," he says, "but time is not on our side. Not only does the earth grow more damaged, but others will seek to stop you."

"Like the man on the road?"

"You were attacked in your village because Eze Udo has uncovered signs of Oala's child. I have a watcher inside the palace. They tell me that the king has learned part of the truth," the griot says. "Enough to know about your connection. The young guard who spared the infant was given another memory as a safeguard—showing how we had overpowered him and taken the child—so his complicity was not revealed. But that is why they came for you. As I said, your destiny is tied with that of Oala's heir."

"Must I go alone?" I ask with a trembling voice.

He sighs. "I wish I could go with you, but my health is not what it was. No one else knows what I will tell you and no one else can know. After what happened with Nduka, I cannot risk it. Not even Ndidi knows the way to the tower."

"How will I protect myself?" I ask.

"As you have done so far," Uchendu says. "You must be careful and stay far from the well-traveled paths. The bush and the rocks will shelter you. The goddess is on our side."

I am still unsure, but I try to be brave. "Where must I go?"

"The tower is in the Stone Hills, far north of the lake and near the edge of the Zare, the great desert. The hills rise to the sky, so finding them will not be a problem. Your challenge is to locate the tower. Tell me, how were you able to find this temple?"

I tell him about the aggri stone Ebele gave me.

"Ah yes, an old tool, but effective. The hole in the rock was made by water, etching through the stone over time. Running water has the power to clear away all impurities and focus our eyes beyond what is normally visible. That is why we built our temple on this lake. When you look through the stone, it's like looking at the world without illusions. A useful gift."

"I'm not sure I can do this," I say.

"You seek answers to your past and a way to save our kingdom," Griot Uchendu says. "You will find both in the tower."

Uchendu gets up and pulls a rope on the wall. "For now, go. Rest yourself," he says. "The day after the morrow, it will be time."

After a few moments, Mataye arrives.

Griot Uchendu turns to me again and takes my hands. "I'm sorry, child. I send you on a difficult journey, but it is one that none but you can complete. May Oala guide your steps and give you strength."

I nod, but fear rises in me again. I don't quite know what will come next, but for the sake of everyone in our dying kingdom, I can only try.

CHAPTER 13

THE STONE HILLS

Two days later, Mataye leads me through a back tunnel that exits on a side of the island opposite to where I arrived with my friends. Along with my other belongings, I carry a new bag of provisions, enough for several days of travel.

I say goodbye to Nweke and Lebechi.

"Why do you have to leave?" Lebechi asks. "We only just arrived."

I know they don't understand, and I can't explain. I barely understand myself. I give them both hugs.

"I'll be back. I promise."

"This is where we leave you." Mataye helps me into a little boat that is waiting on the rocky shore. "I hope you find success and are back with us soon."

"I hope so too," I say, my stomach clenching as I get into the boat. As soon as I'm seated, the boat moves. The shore where Mataye and my friends stand grows smaller, until I can barely see the outline of their forms.

I look toward where Uchendu says I should go. The path to the earth child is a secret he alone has kept, until now. I close my eyes and quietly repeat the directions I have memorized. North through the forest . . . along the river's edge . . . to the summit of the Stone Hills.

When the little boat reaches the shore, I hop out and watch in awe as it floats back across the lake.

The forest holds dangers, both human and beast, but it will provide cover and a place for me to hide. The trees rustle, and I try to calm my fears. Light filters through their scattered leaves as I pick up my bag and walk.

I stumble now and again as I cross the uneven terrain. I pause to drink from my waterskin, but despite my growing fatigue, I know I can't stop until nightfall.

In the market of Danel, I sometimes listened to the stories of traders who traveled from town to town across the kingdom. My little corner of Kun, with the Eke River and our yam fields, seems so far away. I wondered at their tales of the shining sea at our southern coast, the mountainous jungles of the west and the northern sands of the Zare, which now creep ever closer to Kun's heart.

When the sun dips below the horizon, I find a little copse of trees and make another nest of leaves. The pile is cool and soft. It smells like earth and moss—a scent I love.

Jackals yip in the night as they hunt; I burrow deeper into my nest, like one of their rodent prey, trying to stay hidden. I say a silent prayer to Oala. Animals are not my only fear.

The Nkume are still searching for me. Now that I know the horrible truth about Eze Udo, I'm more vigilant than ever to stay out of sight.

I don't know when I fall asleep, but eventually I do. It's a fitful rest, and when I wake, my body aches. I can barely see in the dim light. I blink to focus, but a rustle nearby makes me freeze.

I lift my head slowly and I'm face-to-face with a snake!

The black and yellow python is coiled in a ball, its head resting on its middle. When I stir, the snake lifts its head and stares at me with eyes as black as obsidian. In Kun, pythons are revered, but I've never been so close to one. I'm afraid to move.

The snake flicks its tongue at me, and somewhere in my head a voice whispers, "She has heard your prayer. Be brave."

I gasp. Eke the python is Oala's messenger. The snake looks at me a few moments more, then sinuously unwinds its body and slithers into the bush. I sit back and breathe.

The goddess has heard my prayers. I've never doubted Oala's presence, but to receive such a message in return . . . I begin to cry. What else has she heard me pray about over the years? Over the last few days? I wipe my eyes and feel a little less alone.

Finally, with shaking hands, I rise, erase the remnants of my camp, and travel on.

Sometimes I take out my snakeroot. After my encounter with the python, it has a deeper meaning for me. To make sure I'm heading in the right direction, I say, "Guide me!" The rough ball bounces across the dry ground, and I follow.

At last, I see a break in the trees and race to the edge. My heart drops. Griot Uchendu is right. I had no trouble finding the Stone Hills. Their jagged cliffs loom in front of me but are still so far away. I pick up the snakeroot and continue walking.

I cut through the bush and journey along the edge of a dry riverbed, the water long since gone. Although

I see no one, my sense of unease will not go away. On hearing a twig snap or a bird call, I freeze, but no one is ever there.

On the third day, I reach the base of the Stone Hills. I stop at a rocky ledge leading up to the largest of the hills.

Climbing is harder work than anything I have done so far. The ground is steep and rough, making it difficult for me to keep my balance. I skid on some loose rocks and dash my hand badly against a sharp rock. I cry out in pain, and a small streak of blood stains the stone. But I grit my teeth and keep moving.

At the top of the hill, I expect to see the tower, but cresting the summit, I see nothing. I collapse to the ground and try to think about where to go next. Then I remember my aggri stone.

I pull the small stone from my bag and look through the center. I catch my breath.

There had been nothing but rocks and outcrops for leagues around. But as I look through the aggri stone, I see a building looming not far away. Burnt-orange clay rises to the sky. I crane my neck to see the top. A few narrow windows stagger up the rising walls.

I gather myself and walk toward the tower. When I get close, a whoosh of air caresses my skin. As at the griots' temple, an unseen veil drops. I lower the stone, as it isn't needed any longer, and walk over the parched ground and circle the building twice.

There is no door.

How could that be? There must be some way in. I peer closer. The rough clay has no loose bricks to pull or places I can place my feet to climb. I decide to use my aggri stone again, but even still I see no signs of a threshold.

Griot Uchendu said that no one could enter the tower except me. I lift my hand and press it against the warm brick.

A rumbling vibrates through my fingers, and I feel the ground below me shake. Dried mud falls and rearranges itself. I step back. When the noise stops, an arched entrance has formed into the cavernous tower. Dim light reveals a flight of stairs.

I inch forward. The spiral stairway is cast in gloom, the upper steps lit only from the few windows that climb along the tower's walls. The air is stale and dusty. I begin my ascent, and one by one, my footsteps pad up each stair.

The dizzying climb seems never-ending, and my legs begin to ache. There is no rail to keep me from falling, so I stay as close to the wall as I can. I peek out of one of the windows. Even picking star apples in my orchard, I have never been so far from the ground. Despite how high I've climbed, more steps loom above me. Blood pounds in my ears as I think about what I will find at the top.

The last step opens onto a landing. I turn toward a large wooden door. I've seen it before. Like in my dream, a thick board straddles it, preventing it from being opened.

Uchendu told me that my destiny is tied to that of Oala's child. Coming to the tower will give me the answers I have longed for, will tell me who I am. I step closer and lift the board from its slot. Unlike in my dream, it moves, and I set it heavily to the side.

I grasp the door's handle, and its shape fits comfortably into my hand. The cool iron soothes my nerves. I take a breath and push.

The room is nothing like the rest of the tower. The lonely stairs feel abandoned, but this room speaks of home and comfort. A table and chair sit by the window, and a little cot and blanket rest in the corner. On the hearth, a pot bubbles over a low fire; the delicious smells of groundnuts and yams escape. Along the walls, drawings sprawl. Some are simple, like what a young child would make, but others, of trees, hills, and rivers, are more detailed and show great skill. They depict the views from the tower.

A noise in the corner draws my attention. "Hello,"

I say, turning quickly. "Who's here? I mean no harm. I was sent by the griots."

I hear the stirring again. "Hello," I say again more loudly.

A shadow moves in the corner, and I can see the silhouette of a person.

"The griots sent you?" a girl's voice asks.

"Yes. To free you."

The shadow inches forward, tentative and slow. I imagine the girl wondering about whether to believe me. That's what I'd be thinking in her place.

"I can't see you," I say. "I promise you're safe with me."

The girl finally steps out of the shadows and the world swoops around me. I know that face, have known it for a lifetime. Warm brown skin and dark eyes full of wariness and curiosity.

It is my own.

CHAPTER 14

OALA'S CHILD

It's like looking in a mirror.

"You . . . you look like me," I say. "How is that possible?"

The girl walks into the light, and I see that indeed, in every way possible, the girl and I are alike. Her slight frame and careful movements are as familiar to me as my own. I'm stunned when I notice something more.

We have the same crescent birthmark.

"Who are you?" the girl asks, her voice trembling.

"I am Amara." I can't stop staring at her. As similar as we are, we must be twins. The thought unnerves me. Like the taboo against harming snakes, twins are considered a bad omen. I think of my question to Zirachi. *Do you think I am the curse?*

Instead, I ask, "What's your name?"

"My name is Chizoba," the girl replies.

"And you've survived here by yourself?"

"I'm not alone," Chizoba says. "The goddess sent her servants."

I look around the dim room. It is sparsely furnished but comfortable. In the corner I see the altar to Oala and several carved wooden figures. "But there is no one here," I say.

"There is," she says, gesturing to the statues. "The Arusi serve the goddess and have been my guardians. Whenever I'm hungry or in need of anything, they take care of me. Look!" The girl points to the hearth and the pot simmering over the fire. A spoon stirs the stew and then the whole pot floats to the table. Two bowls appear next to it, ready to be filled with the steaming food. A sound that reminds me of a bush cricket's chirp seems to signal us to come eat.

My hand flies to my mouth, and I look more closely at the wooden statues. They are beautifully painted, two women and two men, each posed in an everyday activity. Arusi figures are in every shrine, and I've seen them countless times. It is said that their intercessions and wisdom help guide the marketplace, community, and all parts of village life. I always thought them symbolic of the goddess watching over us. I shake my head in wonder.

"And why have you come?" Chizoba asks. I shift my attention back to her.

"The griots sent me. They said it's time for you to return, and I'm the only who can bring you."

Chizoba reaches out and hesitantly touches the crescent-shaped birthmark on my neck, identical to her own.

"We're so alike," she whispers.

"Yes," I agree.

"And what will I find in the outside world?"

"Danger," I say. "Leaving won't be safe. There are people who want to hurt you. Hurt us both."

Chizoba frowns and walks over to the window. "All my life I've dreamed of leaving this tower. Now you tell me that if I do, I'll be in danger? I can't say it sounds appealing." She looks back with a wry smile.

I join her. "No, it's not." I wait, then say, "Do you *want* to leave?"

"More than anything," Chizoba says. "I only know what's in this room. Every part of this tower." She looks back out of the window again. "Kun is the unknown. I don't know if I'm ready for it."

"I'll help you," I say.

Chizoba smiles. "I like you, Amara. You make me feel less scared."

I reach for Chizoba's hand. We walk to the table and scoop the groundnut stew into our bowls. Chizoba seems more ravenous for information than she does for the meal.

"I want to hear about your home," she says. "What is it like?"

"I lived on a farm near the Eke River," I say. "We grew yams, and our star apple grove grew the most delicious fruit you'll ever taste." My eyes start to sting, and I blink fast.

"Who is *we*?" Chizoba asks.

"I lived with Zirachi, my adopted mother," I say slowly. "She took care of me."

"A mother," Chizoba says quietly. "Will I get to meet your Zirachi when we leave?"

I shake my head and turn away, wiping the tears I can't blink back. "No. The Ugha, the false ones, killed her. I'm alone now."

"I'm sorry," Chizoba says. She rests her hand on my arm. "You're not alone anymore."

I always thought I'd return to the farm someday. Now I wonder if I should go to the palace with Chizoba. What would it be like to live in the city of

Benta? I can't imagine living away from the sweet fragrance of star apple blossoms in the spring. Then I remember. There may be nothing left after the fire.

I straighten up and wipe my eyes again. "Enough about myself."

We continue to talk. When we leave the table and settle by the fire, I notice in amazement that the bowls clean themselves and the pot returns to the hearth. I have seen more sorcery in the past few days than in my entire life.

We talk about our pasts and ponder the questions that fill us both. I realize that although Chizoba has never left the tower, she has a surprising amount of knowledge. The invisible spirits aren't always silent, she tells me. They tell her stories and describe plants and animals that live in the forest. She can't leave, but they bring objects for her to see and interact with.

Even though we look alike, I also notice differences between Chizoba and me. She bubbles with life, and I think it is not just because she has someone new to talk to. I have grown up with Zirachi and learned her quiet ways. I wonder how Chizoba can be so open and free with someone she has only just met. But whether talking or sitting in comfortable silence, I realize that Chizoba fills something in me that I hadn't known I was missing.

"You should get some rest," I say at last. "We'll begin our journey tomorrow. The griots want us to return as soon as possible."

Chizoba leads me to the little corner where she sleeps, and the Arusi prepare another cot. As we lie down under our blankets, the hearth fire dull and glowing, I know that once we leave the tower, both our lives will change.

CHAPTER 15

THE RETURN

The next morning, we ready ourselves for the journey. The Arusi have laid the table with fresh food and provisions, which we use to stock our bags. Chizoba is quiet, and I can't tell from her expression whether something is troubling her.

As the time grows near, Chizoba stands by the window and looks out.

"I've looked out this window so many times and wondered what was out there," she says. "Now I'm about to leave, and I'm having trouble making my feet move."

"It's okay," I say softly. "I felt the same when I had to leave my home. I was forced, but you have a choice. Whatever you choose, the decision is yours alone—but know that I'll stay with you regardless."

Chizoba looks at me in surprise. "You would do that? Even with everything you told me about the people needing help?"

"Yes," I say. "I can't explain it, but I think Griot Uchendu is right. Our destinies are tied, and where you go, I'll go as well. Neither of us has anyone else truly on our side. In whatever ways Oala has connected us, we're certainly friends."

Chizoba hugs me in a tight embrace.

"If you're willing to stay, then I'm willing to go," she says.

After thanking the Arusi, we feel the rush of the spirits as they leave the tower for good. Chizoba and I walk down the long spiral staircase. They seem less ominous to me now. At the bottom, I pull the old door open, and we both walk into the morning light.

I bound onto the rocky ground first. Chizoba stands in the doorway, apprehension etched on her brow.

"It's all right," I say. "Don't be scared." I reach my hand toward her.

"It's not that," she says. "I was only setting this in my memory. I may never come back, and I want to remember it." From around us, we hear a chirp of encouragement from the Arusi, still watching over

Chizoba in her last moments at the tower. After a pause, she steps out onto the rough ground.

I lead and Chizoba follows, her steps more hesitant. I slow my pace to allow her to gain footing as she begins to navigate this new world.

I have warned Chizoba about our need to stay hidden, and we stay close to the brush and trees when we can. Once, a band of people appear, and we duck into the grass and lie on our stomachs to watch. A man, woman, and three young children. Their thin frames betray their hunger. They remind me of Nweke's lost family, and I wonder if he will ever find his people again. The man struggles to lead their donkey down the road, and I can tell the cart is much too heavy. It must hold everything they own.

After they pass, we carefully rise and walk on. Chizoba and I both know that the threat of capture, or worse, is always near. No words are needed.

Despite my worries, I find the path is easy to retrace. That gives my curiosity free rein.

"Do you have a favorite food?" I ask.

Chizoba shrugs. "I like the vegetable stew that I sometimes prepare. Often, I eat the same meal. Once, the spirits brought some berries from the lake to our south. Those were delicious! I could have eaten them for days, but I only had a small bowl.

"What do you like to do for fun?" she asks me, changing the subject.

"I never had much time for games—we worked in the field and the orchard most of the day, or we sold goods in the market." But then I grin. "Sometimes, when Zirachi gave me leave, I ran with my friend Ifeoma and the other children. We would toss sticks to see who could throw the farthest, or sometimes we played mancala under the trees."

Chizoba's eyes widen. "That sounds wonderful. I never did anything like that." She sighs. "I like to draw and have learned a bit of weaving."

"Chizoba, do you wonder if we're sisters?"

"It would explain our likeness, but why wouldn't they tell us?"

I shake my head. "I wonder if it's because of the taboo against twins. I would have been happy to have a sister."

"As would I."

We fall silent, and I wonder how different our lives would have been if we had grown up together. There's so much I don't understand.

Finally, we find a patch of trees and decide to rest for the night. The nighttime temperature has dropped, and I shiver as I dig into my bag of provisions. I set up a hearth and take out my flint and firestone to create a spark. It's a risk, but I think we are far enough into the bush to avoid being seen.

"What are you doing?" Chizoba asks curiously.

"We need a fire to stay warm tonight."

"I've never had to start one before. How is it done?"

I show Chizoba how to build a nest of tinder and strike the firestone with the flint. Soon we see smoke and a glow, then a flame bursts forth, creating warm, inviting light.

We eat, then gather leaves for our beds. As we lie in the soft piles, the crackling embers lull us and we talk.

"Do you realize that you're a queen?" I ask. "Oala's child is meant to rule Kun, and that's who you are."

"I suppose," Chizoba says, "but it's strange to think about." She looks across the flame at me. "If I'm queen, you must be queen as well," she says. "How could it be any other way when we're so alike?"

"I don't know," I say hesitantly.

"Well, they say you're the only one who could free me. Perhaps the healing of Kun will only take place if we're together."

"I still don't understand how going to the capital will stop Eze Udo. He has the Ugha and Nkume at his service. They're too powerful."

Chizoba casts her gaze at the flickering light. "We must be ready to defend ourselves when we go to Benta. Eze Udo won't stand aside."

For the first time, I think about what's coming. War seems inevitable now that Chizoba has laid out the problem so plainly.

A twig snaps a few steps away, and I sit up. I now notice how quiet it has become. I no longer hear the whistle of bush owls or the rustle of grasshoppers in the darkness. Chizoba sits up too, my wariness spreading to her.

As my eyes strain, trying to make sense of the gloom, I hear a faint noise again and know it was a mistake to light a fire. I kick dirt over the embers to smother their light.

"Come!" I urge Chizoba. "We need to go."

Even as the words come out of my mouth, I know it's too late. Arms wrap around me, and I'm lifted from the ground.

"Amara!" I hear Chizoba cry out. Then she too rises, and a hand covers her mouth. We reach toward each other, our fingertips barely touching. I have trouble breathing, and darkness closes in from the sides.

I fall into nothingness.

CHAPTER 16

KING AND CURSE

My head is groggy, and I'm floating. As I become more alert, I realize that I'm over someone's shoulder and my hands and feet are bound. I look to my side and see Chizoba, unconscious, over the shoulder of another person. Our captors are wearing red cloaks—these are the Nkume.

Panic takes hold. What do they want? They tried to take me before and killed Zirachi to do it.

"You're awake," says a voice that I know. I can't see him, but I remember what he looks like. Black hair, dark brown skin, and the amber eyes I knew in another.

"I didn't think I would see you again so soon," Okwu says in a low whisper. "I still haven't thanked you properly for the scar you gave me."

I try to kick—to make him drop me. I don't know what I'll do if he does, though. Running is impossible with my legs tied, but I must get to Chizoba.

"Stop it," Okwu hisses. "There's no point in that. No one is going to hurt you. Eze Udo would like the honor of your presence."

My heart freezes. Chizoba and I are being taken to Benta. There is only one purpose the king could have in mind—to finish the task at which he failed twelve seasons ago.

I decide to save my energy. Even if I can free myself, I can't get to Chizoba, and I won't leave her. To be honest, I want to see Eze Udo again. He ordered the death of the one person who loved me, and I want to know why.

After what seems like hours of walking, we're put down and our feet are untied.

"Commander Nduka," Okwu says with a nod as a man approaches us. I realize with a start that it is the Ugha who attacked me and Zirachi on the road from Danel, the man with the flute. The name lingers in my thoughts until I remember why I know it. He was Griot Uchendu's apprentice—before he left to follow Eze Udo.

"From here, you'll walk," Nduka growls. "You'll

follow every direction you're given." Chizoba and I look at each other, our eyes wide with fear.

We trudge along the road. Commander Nduka leads the way, and Nkume guards flank us in front and behind.

Around the last bend, the road widens, and before us looms a huge city. I've heard of the walls of Benta, but they are grander than I had imagined. Huge mud bricks, stacked almost as high as Chizoba's tower, surround the city. Watchtowers rise in several places all along its perimeter, and I see more soldiers positioned along the ramparts. Muted banners flap listlessly in the dusty air, as we enter the enormous main gate. I feel like I am marching into the maw of a beast.

Within the city, it reminds me of Danel. Or rather, what my village has become.

A group of thin children pull a stubborn goat by a rope through the dust. A woman pounds grain in a bowl, wiping away her sweat with the back of her hand. A sickly beggar crouches under a leaning palm tree, stretching his hands out for charity. No one stops.

Any joy the people once had has been replaced with fear and desperation. I understand why Nweke and his family left.

We pass rows of shops and homes. People see us and quickly duck inside and close their reed doors. Marching farther into the city, I see that Benta isn't just one city, but a collection of smaller ones. I have no desire to marvel at its construction, knowing where we are going.

Before long, we reach the top of the high street and the castle. More guards are stationed by the entrance, and the tall doors open on our approach.

We walk into a great hall. A large throne stands at the end of the room, a set of carved steps leading up to the platform. From his seat, the king watches us, his brown eyes piercing.

"Eze Udo, we bring you the girls," says Commander Nduka.

Udo wears robes of red and gold this time, but the black glove I noticed before still covers his right hand. He looks at us with keen interest that only mildly hides his distaste.

"Remarkable," he says almost to himself. "I hope your journey was comfortable."

"It wasn't," I say.

"Such spirit for one so young." His eyes narrow as he considers my stubborn and angry face. "We'll see how long that spirit will hold." Eze Udo then

118

turns to Chizoba. "And you . . . Have you no venom to spit my way?"

"Why are you doing this?" she replies. "We've done nothing."

"Not yet," Udo says, "but I have no doubt that you mean to help yourselves to what I have earned."

"What do you mean?" I ask. "We only want to help our people—fix what's broken in the land."

"Broken?" The king laughs. "How interesting that you say that. I want to do that too."

My skin prickles when he says this, and I doubt he means it the same way I do.

"Do you know how I came to be king?"

"We know Eze Ikemba entrusted you to take care of the kingdom until his heir was born. Instead, you took the throne for yourself," I say.

"I ended the yoke of tyranny this kingdom has suffered under. Our kings and queens were foisted on us by the gods. We allowed them to rule out of fear. I was not afraid and brought the throne back to our control."

"I saw you in Danel offering thanks to the goddess," I say.

"For the people. For show," he says, with a wave of scorn.

I didn't think my dislike for the man could grow, but I see now that he believes in no one and nothing but himself.

"But why did you try to hurt Chizoba?" I ask. "She's done you no harm."

"No harm?" Udo says, glancing at his gloved hand. "It seems the griots have not told you the truth." Udo stands and comes down the steps toward us. "My griots foresaw the same signs that the others had and knew the arrival of Oala's child was at hand. I would not let another usurper come to the throne, so I sent the Nkume to find the child." His eyes lock with Chizoba's.

"They found the infant, a girl, swaddled in sweet-grass in the woods. While the Nkume and my griots fought with Uchendu, I approached the child. I had learned of a song which would cut away its powers and transfer them to me. Then our kingdom would have a true Eze, born of *this* world, but with the power to provide the abundance we needed."

"You mean you tried to steal magic from a baby," I say.

He turns to me. "I would warn you to show more respect. Do you know what the penalty for treason is?"

"You don't scare us," says Chizoba, holding her chin up.

"But I should," he says. "When I found the child, I needed to do more than take magic. For its power to be transferred, its life would have to be forfeited as well."

The hideousness of Udo's act hangs in the air.

"Your plan failed," I say.

The king pauses. "I wouldn't say failed," he says. "Rather, there were unexpected consequences." My chest tightens. "As I chanted the words, a surge of light blasted me back and did this." He raises his hand and removes the glove, revealing jagged white scars racing along the brown skin of his hand and palm. "I was injured and in pain, but I intended to finish my plan. When I neared the rubble, I saw not one child, but two."

"Two? Another earth child was born?" Even as I say it, my mind unravels the truth.

"No. The power of the child rebounded and tore it apart." Eze Udo looks at me with scorn. "When you look at each other, you are looking at your other half."

My legs feel weak, and Chizoba and I lock eyes.

In Udo's horrible words, the truth remains. The

bond we feel. We are one person in *two* bodies.

I don't know how to feel. I care about Chizoba, but how can we be the same person?

Eze Udo replaces his glove and returns to his throne. He looks at the two of us.

"I knew if you both lived, you would still be a threat to me. I drew my sword to end you both. How I wish I had," he says without remorse.

"Why didn't you?" Chizoba asks. Her eyes refuse to leave the king's.

"The griots found us and drove us back. Then Uchendu magicked you away," he says, gesturing at Chizoba. "Fortunately, my guard was able to take you to finish the job I had started." He looks at me. "When he returned from the forest, I thought the job was done. Until I saw a little girl in Danel who had a particular crescent-shaped mark." Eze Udo reclines on his throne, satisfaction relaxing his frown. "King Ikemba had the same mark. So, I discovered the trick the griots had played. They hid you well, but not well enough."

"So do you mean to kill us?" I ask, afraid to hear his answer. My whole world has been rocked.

"Eventually," he says. "I have had twelve seasons to think about what went wrong. At first, I just wanted you gone, but with both of you alive, I have another plan. My griots assure me that there is a way to regain what I lost."

A sick feeling creeps into my stomach, and I inch closer to Chizoba.

"We can repair that which has been torn apart."

"You mean," I say, glancing at Chizoba, "put us back together?"

"When you are whole, your powers will be restored," Udo says.

"What will happen to us?" I say.

"I don't care," the king says, with no emotion in his dark eyes. "You'll be no more when I have what I need. It matters not to me how and when it happens." Eze Udo waves his gloved hand as if swatting a gnat. "We've learned from our mistakes. This time I *will* succeed."

"Oala will protect us!" Chizoba cries.

"I doubt that, little one," Udo says. "The song will be sung when day turns to night. Until then, I offer you the comfort of my dungeons." He claps his hands, and two Nkume guards roughly grab us and drag us away.

With a spear at our backs, we walk through the shadowy corridors of the castle following the guard in front of us. Our footsteps echo as we march through the grimy halls.

My head spins with all that I have learned. I am Oala's daughter. I am broken.

I hear Chizoba sniffling next to me. As overwhelmed as I feel, I can hardly imagine what this is like for her, who has only known solitude and safety. I reach out my hand, and she takes it. We tighten our fingers together. Even if we were meant to be one person, we are two girls now. Two lives. Two hearts. Two wills to live.

We descend the dank and musty stairs to the lowest level of the dungeon and pass several cells. Some hold muttering prisoners who stare through their iron bars at us. The place is foul-smelling, and stinks of filth and rotting food. I dare to look in one cell and see a man shaking, curled up in the corner. Is that how this will end for Chizoba and me? As we march on, I wonder how far below ground Udo plans to lock us up.

Finally, we turn a corner and come to an empty block of cells. My throat tightens. We stop near one, and I think the guard in front will open the door and shove us in. Instead, he crouches.

"What is going on?" I ask.

"Quiet," he whispers, continuing to feel the rough stones with his hands.

"What are you doing?"

"Helping you," says Okwu, whose voice I now recognize. He pushes a small stone at the base of the wall. There is a click, and I hear metal grind. Next to us, a drainage grate moves to reveal a narrow tunnel.

"I can't make it through here, but you can," he says. After you enter, I'll shut the grate. Move as fast as you can. It leads to the underwater river. You can wade through, and I'll meet you at the other end, where it opens to the forests, and I can get you out.

"How can we trust you?" I ask in disbelief. "You tried to kill me."

"No," he says wryly. "I am the reason you're still alive." Okwu raises his head toward a sound. Boots echo in the distance. "You must go now."

I am about to ask more questions when the other guard removes his helmet. I stare at a face that I only see in my dreams now.

It is Zirachi.

"Amara," she says urgently. "We go. Now!"

CHAPTER 17

GHOST IN THE NIGHT

It is like seeing a ghost. I remember Zirachi struggling for breath in the grip of the Ugha's conjuring. I see Mango's carcass lying in the ashen road and listen to Ebele's report about the smoking ruins of my home.

"How can this be?" I ask as I stare at my mother, looking so strange in the garb of a soldier.

"I'll explain everything," Zirachi says, "but we must move quickly. Go into the tunnel, and don't make a sound." Zirachi gently pushes Chizoba and me through the opening and climbs in after us. As soon as she is through, Okwu closes the grate and crouches down again to speak to us.

"Remember, follow this tunnel to the end, and you'll come to where it flows from the city and down toward the river. You'll see other passageways that lead to other parts of the city. Follow this one. I'll meet you at the other end as soon as I can. Once they realize you're gone, the alarm will be raised and there'll be a thorough search. By that point, they'll also notice that I'm missing and may begin to put the pieces together. Now go and stay safe!"

Zirachi puts her fingers through the bars and grips Okwu's hand. He gives her a tight smile and then is gone.

"Come," Zirachi whispers sharply, and takes the lead. We splash through the filthy water of the tunnel. As we slosh, I hear squeaks and skittering from the walls. In the murk, our only guides are our ears and the half-light that sometimes filters from the ceiling grates above us. We stay to the tunnel's edge to keep as dry as possible. I stumble on a branch and imagine it's a hand reaching out to grab me. Foul debris floats in the water. A rat clings to a pile of flotsam and stares at us with hungry eyes.

Soon the tunnel narrows, and we must venture into the water. Cold grips my body and my teeth rattle from the chill. As we wade, Zirachi glances back to make sure we are keeping up. Chizoba has never been in water and struggles more than me to hold her balance as we progress. I burn with questions for Zirachi and try to speak, but Zirachi shoots her finger to her lips, insisting I stay silent. She points up at another grate, and I understand. The echo of the tunnels will carry any sound we make and signal that someone is below. I nod and hold my tongue.

Instead, I wonder about how Zirachi is alive! I also puzzle over Okwu's actions. He threw me into the Eke River and tried to drown me.

Or did he?

As I replay the moment in my head, I see myself lashing out with Zirachi's dagger and cutting him across the cheek. I remember the tight grip of his hand on my clothing as he lifts me off the ground and dangles me over the river. Udo said he sent the Nkume to retrieve me and Chizoba. If Okwu was meant to bring us to the city, why did he throw me into the river? I thought it was in vengeance, but what if it wasn't? Did he try to save me?

Confusion swirls in my head. The tunnel branches and the passages that Okwu spoke of join with ours, making the water grow from a stream to a shallow river. We wade toward the side to stay in the shadows. Finally, I see a large gate.

Zirachi grabs the bars and mimics the high-pitched call of a wood owl, like the ones that nest in our star apple trees. She waits and repeats the call. Nothing. She waves for us to stay against the wall of the tunnel and looks furtively into the dark. Something is wrong.

Okwu said he would meet us at the other end of the passage, but he isn't here. What if our disappearance has been discovered more quickly than planned?

Zirachi shakes the bars, apparently hoping one might pull free, but the metal is solid from top to bottom.

Chizoba and I yank at them too, but it is no use. I have an idea, though. I take a breath and plunge into the dark water, keeping my hands on the rungs of the grate to feel my way to its base. When I feel the floor of the tunnel, I use my other hand to begin exploring. As I move along, I suddenly feel a narrow gap.

I stand up, gasping in the dank air. Zirachi wades over and grabs my shoulders angrily. I point down to show that I found a way out. She looks hesitant, then takes a breath and goes down herself. After a moment, she returns, her face confirming she has found the gap too. I turn to Chizoba.

"We must go under the bars. It's the only way," I whisper.

Chizoba's eyes are wide with apprehension, but I wade to her and take her hand. "You can do it. I know you can."

"I'll go first and try to raise the grate," Zirachi says.

"No." I grab her arm. "I'll go. I'm smaller and can pass through more easily." Zirachi looks unsure but I squeeze again. "I can do it." She finally nods.

I slosh back to the grate and take another breath.

The water prickles my skin as I move my hands down the bars to the gap. At the bottom, I flip onto my back. I turn my head sideways to fit through the narrow space, then wiggle my frame under the bars. Halfway through, my clothes snag.

My lungs burn as I fumble with my skirt. I tug harder, but I can't get it loose. Air bubbles escape from my nose, and I feel dizzy and extremely tired. It feels good to close my eyes for just a moment.

Suddenly, hands tug at my waist, and someone pushes my legs under the grate. I kick up and stagger to my feet.

My first ragged breath burns, and I sputter water. As my dizziness clears, I see Chizoba's frightened face on the other side of the grate.

"Are you all right?" she whispers. "You were under so long."

The water erupts, and Zirachi appears next to

Chizoba, pulling up on the bars as she catches her breath.

"Okay?" she asks.

I nod and try to calm my pounding heart. I wade over to the bars and feel the stones along the wall. There must be a trigger, like the one Okwu used to open the other grate. At last, a stone moves when I push it, and I hear a grinding click. But the bars don't raise. I grab hold and tug. Zirachi and Chizoba help and soon we can lift the grate enough for them to squeeze under.

Chizoba comes through, splashing in her panic. I grab her and help her get her balance. A few moments later, Zirachi surfaces too.

She points to the side of the river, and we pull ourselves onto the muddy bank next to the city wall. As we sit dripping, I close my eyes. We're out, but now what? The Nkume will be looking for us. Nowhere seems safe.

Zirachi decides. Putting her fingers to her lips, she beckons us to follow her. She runs along the end of the wall. I look up and see shadows moving above. Watchmen. When Zirachi gets to a part of the wall that is closest to the tree cover, she pulls me forward and points up and then to the trees. I understand. I need to watch above to make sure a guard isn't passing when I make my dash for the tree line. I watch. When they move away from their spot, I dash for the tree cover. I pant as I lay against the rough bark.

After what seems like eons, Chizoba runs over, and I grab her by her arm.

"Oh!" she says. Her eyes are filled with fear until she recognizes me.

We huddle and wait for Zirachi to come. As moments pass, a knot clenches in my stomach. I wonder if I should go back, and start to move, but Chizoba stops me. "No, we have to wait."

"But what if something is wrong?" I ask.

"Zirachi told me if she didn't make it to our side in a few minutes, we should keep going. She'll catch up to us."

I don't respond. We won't leave without Zirachi. I lost her once, and it's only through Oala's grace that I have her back.

Finally, Zirachi bursts through the tree cover. She bends over to catch her breath. "We need to go. There was a changing of the guard, so I couldn't move, but Eze Udo will want a report soon. We must put distance between us and this place before that happens. Someone will lose their head, and I don't wish it to be me."

Zirachi looks back at the city, and I know that she is worried about Okwu.

"Don't worry, I'm sure he will find us," I say.

"He will," she replies quietly, and then leads us through the forest path.

CHAPTER 18

PAST AND FUTURE

We are silent for the longest time, our hearts pounding and ears straining for any sounds of pursuit.

Zirachi leads us through the woods, never traveling in one direction too long before veering a different way. At last, she slows and leans against a tree to catch her breath. I do what I have wanted to do from the moment I recognized her. I run over to Zirachi and hug her tight, letting my tears fall freely.

Zirachi doesn't hold back her emotions either this time. She wraps her arms around me and rocks me back and forth.

"I was so scared," I say into the folds of Zirachi's cloak. "I thought you were dead, and I was all alone."

"Shhh . . ." Zirachi says as she strokes my braids

and holds me tighter. "I know," she says. "I looked for you, but you had already been sent on your quest by the griots. She puts her fingers under my chin and tilts it up. Looking into my puffy eyes, she says, "I'm so proud of you. You're everything I hoped you would be and more."

"Me? I haven't done anything."

"Yes, you have. You've brought us hope. You're braver than you ever thought you could be." She reaches her hand out to Chizoba, who stands shyly to the side. "And you," Zirachi says, "come here."

Chizoba comes over, and Zirachi wraps her into the folds of her cloak too. "You are my daughter as well."

We all hold tight, never wanting to let go, but we finally do. Zirachi gestures for us to rest on a fallen trunk. She removes her water pouch and lets us all take small sips.

"I don't understand how you're alive," I say.

Zirachi laughs as she puts the pouch away. "I have pondered that question many times myself," she says. "It's all due to Okwu."

"How?" I ask in surprise.

"I know so much more about my brother than I did before. I understand why he kept away now. I was angry for many years, but I know now that he did it for us both." She pauses, and her expression is serious. "He didn't leave me behind," she says.

Chizoba and I both look puzzled, so Zirachi continues.

"Twelve seasons ago, when Eze Udo sent his Ugha to hunt for Oala's child, Okwu was a young guard. Our parents taught us to revere the goddess, and Okwu recognized the evil of Udo's plan. He secretly pledged to help the griots protect the child."

"He couldn't stop Udo from singing his song, but when it failed, Okwu volunteered to find and kill you, Amara. Instead, he took you back to the griots. He told them about his home and suggested that Amara be brought to me. Okwu killed a bush rabbit and the griots then used their song so that he would recall killing you instead.

"Chizoba was taken to the safety of the tower. With you separated and hidden, the griots hoped Eze Udo would never be able to gain the power he sought. And, Amara," Zirachi says quietly, "you already know part of this tale. One night, I opened my door to find a basket holding a weak and sickly babe. I vowed to keep her safe and raise her as my own." Zirachi wipes her eyes. "I've tried my best."

Here are the answers that I long for. Having them feels good, but more importantly, they strengthen what I know to be true: Zirachi is my family. She always has been.

"How did Okwu help you escape the Ugha?" Chizoba asks.

"I knew nothing of what had become of Okwu since he'd left home. When I saw him in Danel, he wasn't the brother I remembered. But after Amara escaped to the river, the Ugha wanted no witness, and I was tied up and left in the burning house. Okwu dragged me out the rear. He told me what happened at the river and begged me to trust him. He had to go back with the Nkume, but I was to follow his directions and go to the griots. He gave me his masquerade mask—You remember, Amara. The one in the shape of a leopard. I used it as a disguise until I was safe."

"I never want to leave you again, Zirachi," I say.

"I wish the same," she says, wrapping her arms around both Chizoba and me.

"But we're still not safe," Chizoba says. "Udo wants to bind us together."

"Yes. I heard about that." Zirachi hesitates. "It would be the life that was stolen from you," she says quietly.

I am shocked. "All I know about this 'binding' is that there will no longer be two of us. How can it be right if we both give up our lives?"

Chizoba and I look at each other. It sometimes feels as if we can read each other's thoughts.

"There must be another way," I say.

Zirachi tilts her head. "I'm no griot, but I trust them. They've tried to keep you both safe. Udo means you harm, and I won't let that happen. I don't want to lose either of you. The griots will know what to do."

Zirachi stands up and looks around in the dimming light. "I wish I knew where Okwu was," she whispers. I know she is thinking of her bitter words to Okwu and doesn't want to leave him, but at last she says, "It's not safe. Girls, we should go."

We reach a clear stream, which is a blessed sight. The murk of Benta's river has stuck our clothes to our bodies. I still recall the rat that we saw in the water, and it makes my skin crawl. We wade in and scrub our skin and hair to get clean. When we are finished, the damp clothes still cling to our skin, but that feels so much more pleasant than having the filth of the city on us.

Zirachi looks behind more frequently once we travel on. She finally pauses and whispers, "Someone's following us." My nerves are raw. What if the Ugha have tracked us down?

Zirachi finally waves us under an overhang of

rock, hidden from view, while she gets behind a tree. I see Zirachi pull out a dagger and hold it close. Her brow is etched with worry. Suddenly, I hear the slight tread of boots, and I push Chizoba against the roughness of the stone.

When the footsteps reach Zirachi, she flings herself forward and presses her knife to the man's throat.

"It's you!" she says in relief. Okwu is tense but happy to see us. Chizoba and I run from our hiding place.

"Yes. I wasn't sure I would make it out," he says. "The king knows we're gone and is already tracking us. We must move."

We increase our pace. Okwu says there is no time and the most direct route is our only hope of reaching the protection of the griots.

I run up to Okwu. "I'm sorry I cut you," I say. "I thought you were trying to hurt me." It's hard to change the picture I have of him in my mind.

Okwu smiles, tilting his head so I can see the cut on his face. The fiery slit I remember curves across his cheek but has faded to a thin red line.

"There are some who would say I have more character now," he says. "I'm sure I can think of a thrilling story to go along with it to charm the women of the court."

"Or a certain griot," Zirachi says with a smile. Okwu ignores her.

"I think the real story is thrilling enough," I say.

"That it might be," he says. "I know you meant no harm, and I'm sorry I scared you. I knew that if you fell into Udo's hands, I might not be able to help. In the river, you had a chance."

"You were right," I reply.

We reach the lake and even though we see nothing there, I know the griots' temple stands at the center.

Okwu moves to the water's edge and says, "I seek the truth!"

The rush of water reveals stepping stones, as before. One after another, we move silently across the water.

CHAPTER 19

ADDER IN THE GRASS

Once on the rocky shore, we follow Okwu to the huge doors. They open upon our approach.

Mataye, Griot Ndidi, Nweke, and Lebechi greet us in the hall.

"Welcome back!" Mataye says. "We knew you would succeed in your quest."

Chizoba seems overwhelmed by the new surroundings, and Griot Ndidi approaches her. "Welcome to you, Chizoba. We've waited for your return for a long time." She turns back to me. "For both of you."

Mataye gives Okwu and Zirachi hearty handshakes. "Well done to you both." Okwu nods to Ndidi, who smiles broadly.

I run to my friends and hug them. They look so

different. Nweke wears a simple tunic and pants, not unlike Mataye's. His and Lebechi's faces are bright and full.

"I missed you both. How are you?"

"Very well," Nweke says. "The griots are kind. We searched for my family, but they're gone. I'm going to be an apprentice now."

"And Griot Ndidi is teaching me how to read," Lebechi chimes in. "I'm so glad you're back."

I lead them to the other girl. "Meet Chizoba. She's my . . ." I hesitate. "Me!" I say at last.

Chizoba smiles, but Lebechi leaps forward and hugs her around the waist. "Now I have two of you!" she says happily.

Mataye interrupts our greetings. "Please follow me. The griots require your presence, and time is growing short."

Chizoba and I take each other's hands again and follow Mataye and Griot Ndidi. This walk is so different. I don't feel like the same girl who arrived from Danel. Indeed, I'm not. What I knew about my life was not the whole truth, and now there are so many questions I want to ask Griot Uchendu.

I also fear what he'll ask Chizoba and me to do.

Mataye opens the wooden doors, and we enter the great hall. There are several griots talking with each other. Griot Uchendu sits at the table waiting—apparently for us.

"Teacher," Mataye says, "they've arrived."

"Thank you," the griot replies, and beckons for us all to have a seat. "Come, children," he says to Chizoba and me. "I want to see you."

We approach the griot.

"I will not harm you," he says kindly to Chizoba. "Having you both here means we are one step closer to repairing the kingdom."

He stares between each of us. "It is a blessing from the Mother that you are here. Eze Udo used evil magic to strip away your powers, and the entire kingdom has paid the cost.

"Why didn't you tell me the truth?" I ask.

"I did tell you the truth," he says gently. "I only said what would make sense to you at the time. Sometimes knowledge given at the wrong time can be dangerous."

"Is there anything you're not telling us now?" Chizoba asks warily.

He sighs, and I sense he is trying to choose his words carefully.

"In order to restore Kun to health, your powers must be restored. They were driven out of you by the curse."

"But not completely," I interrupt. "The Ugha couldn't harm me with his magic. You also said that only I could find Chizoba. When I found her tower, touching the clay wall opened a door."

"You are right. You both have traces of magic that could not be erased."

He looks at us more seriously. "But that is not enough for what comes next. The truth is that our world is withering away, and Udo does not recognize it. Rather, he does not recognize his role in it. He knows that he needs Oala's magic to restore what he has broken, and that has made him more desperate than ever to have you both. But he is right. You were meant to exist as one and were split by his curse. The binding song will reunify you—body and spirit. Once complete, your powers to heal Kun should also be restored."

"But that sounds no different than what Udo wants to do." I look at Chizoba, who nods. "We don't want to give up who we are, especially for only a *chance* at repairing our world. We want to stay together, but as ourselves. Wouldn't two of us be more powerful than one against Udo?"

Okwu looks on quietly, but Zirachi puts her hand on my shoulder. Her gentle touch reassures me.

Uchendu pauses before he speaks. "There is a

chance. Without the rebinding, you will not be as strong; but if you are set on your decision, we'll do what we can."

"There must be another way to return our abilities," Chizoba says.

"Rebinding would undo the evil that has been done. All that was stripped away would be returned, and you would be strong enough to protect yourself from Udo. As a baby, you could not do that, but you could wield that power now to protect yourself and others." He stands up and begins to pace. When he turns back, he says, "But there is a song that may help reconnect you with the earth's powers. You may have enough latent magic to make it possible. With time, you might develop the strength to push back the Zare."

"And this song would allow us to stay as ourselves?" I ask.

"It would."

"Then that is what we will do," Chizoba says.

"And we can protect them from Udo," Okwu says, glancing at his sister. Zirachi smiles.

The old griot takes Chizoba's hand and mine. "You both have been asked to take on much and have great wisdom for your age," he says. "Perhaps it is time we learn from you."

He turns to Ndidi and the other griots in the room. "We need to study the song and prepare to do it quickly. Let our guests get food and rest, and we will commence at dusk."

Griot Uchendu extends his hand toward the door for us.

"Okwu and Zirachi, please stay. I have need of your assistance. Mataye, can you take the girls to their room to rest?"

Mataye beckons us to follow him. We wave goodbye to the others. He leads us down the hall to the same room that I stayed in before.

"There's food on the table by the window, and you may rest until my teacher is ready for you.

We thank him and shut the door.

I sit on the bed, and Chizoba walks to the little table where fruit, bread and nuts, and some little cakes have been set out. Chizoba takes a cake and turns it in her hands.

"Did we make the right decision?" I ask.

Chizoba nods. "I think so. We can still help this way. If we did the rebinding, I am afraid of what it would mean for us."

"I know," I say. "I think about my friends Nweke and Lebechi. They were so hungry and alone when I met them. It's better now, but there are so many others in need." I breathe deeply. "We could make life better for everyone."

"Griot Uchendu says the other way could work also," Chizoba says.

"Yes, perhaps. I hope it will be enough."

Chizoba lifts the cake to her mouth and takes a bite. I go to take some food as well. "That looks good!" I pick up the other cake and raise it to my lips, but Chizoba knocks it away.

In shock, I see that her lips are blue. She makes a horrible gasp and falls to the floor.

"Chizoba!" I scream. I drop to the floor and shake her. "What is it?" I cry. Chizoba's eyes are open wide, and she struggles to breathe.

I run to the door. "Help! Help me!"

Footsteps run down the corridor. Okwu and Zirachi enter first, followed by Griot Ndidi and others. Mataye comes too and stands in the doorway, his eyes fixed on the scene.

"What happened?" Zirachi asks, kneeling next to Chizoba, who is starting to shake.

"She bit into that cake. I started to eat it too, but she knocked it from my hand," I cry.

Zirachi looks at a loss, but then Uchendu pushes into the room and kneels next to Chizoba. He puts his face close to hers. "This girl has been poisoned," he says sternly. "There is uchichi seed on her breath. He turned sharply toward the others in the room. "Where did this food come from?"

No one answers, but I notice Mataye is gone.

Chizoba's gasping grows louder, and I turn back to her.

"Please," I plead with Uchendu, "help her. There must be an antidote." Tears fall freely down my cheeks as I hold Chizoba's hands. She looks at me, her eyes full of fear, but unable to speak.

Uchendu kneels by our sides. "I cannot stop the poison," he says softly.

Chizoba coughs violently and struggles for breath. The rise and fall of her chest slows.

"We could do the binding," I say suddenly.

Zirachi looks at me in surprise. "Amara, no!"

"Will it save her?" I ask Uchendu.

"It is possible," he says, "but there is not much time."

"Do it," I say, my voice harsh. I will not let Chizoba die without doing everything in my power.

"Are you sure?" Zirachi asks quietly, resting her hand on mine.

"Yes."

Uchendu takes my hand in his and Chizoba's in

his other. He places our palms together, and we clasp our fingers tightly.

Ndidi and the other griots surround us and lay their hands on Uchendu as he murmurs words I don't understand. As the sun greets the horizon outside the window, a warmth radiates from my fingers and creeps up my arm. Chizoba's eyes widen; she feels it too. The griots continue to sing, low and strong, and soon light emanates from between Chizoba and me.

Zirachi and Okwu move back as the light becomes more intense. What began as a warmth now is uncomfortable, painful. I flinch but don't pull away. The light burns like lightning in my veins, but I know this is the only way to save Chizoba.

There is a crack and a flash of light.

Uchendu and the other griots fall back. Okwu runs forward to help the old man to stand.

Zirachi cautiously moves closer. Where two of us had lain moments before, there is only one. The floor is blasted and cracked around me.

"Amara?" Zirachi asks hesitantly.

I lift my head slowly and look at her.

"My name is Amarachi."

CHAPTER 20

SACRIFICES

I stand up, unsteady on my feet. My hands, my body, feel the same as before, but something is different. It vibrates in the air around me.

"Amarachi," Zirachi says. "Do you know me?"

I cautiously step forward, but she runs to me, and I wrap my arms around her. "I could never forget you, Zirachi." She hugs me tightly, but I feel a tremble in her embrace.

"It is me," I say, looking up at her. "I remember our life on the farm. Danel. Our friends." But then I hesitate. "But I also remember living in the tower. I remember how happy I was when I met Amara—I mean me." I struggle to find the words to express my tangle of thoughts and feelings.

Griot Uchendu approaches. "Little one, the next few days will be disorienting for you. You have the memories of two people to assimilate into one. At times they will seem separate from you, but you will find that they are not. They are you."

I look at him seriously. "Thank you for saving Chizoba's life." I think about it again. "My life."

"I did what you asked," Uchendu says. "A sacrifice made in love is stronger than anything Eze Udo can conjure."

"What do you mean?"

"Those with power are often lured by their own selfish desires. That is what led Udo to usurp the throne. He convinces himself it is for the good of the people, but he is consumed by envy and bitterness. Instead of helping the people, he has hurt us badly."

"And for that, he should be punished," I say. I have never felt this way before, such anger. Under the surface, I feel my emotions fluctuate, threatening to overtake the thoughts I still try to sort out. I don't know myself, and it scares me.

Ndidi takes my hand. It is warm and steady.

"Sometimes it is not our desire to go astray, but if we step off the right path, it becomes harder to find our way back," she says. "Remember who you are, Amarachi. Our people need you."

I think I understand the warning, but I don't know how to do that yet. I feel my love for Zirachi and my friends. But the desire to avenge myself on Udo clouds my thoughts. I know that stopping the Zare should be my goal. My anger subsides but doesn't go away.

"I must call a council to tell the others what has happened," Griot Uchendu says. "It is imperative that we start your training. Now that you have access to your powers, we're not safe until you learn to control them."

I look at Zirachi and Okwu and can see apprehension in their eyes.

"I would never hurt anyone," I say.

"We know," Zirachi says.

"But," says the griot, "magic wielded without knowledge or care can be a bigger threat than Udo or his Ugha. Let us make our plans."

Three days have passed since the binding. The griots hold a small ceremony in the great hall to recognize me as Eze Nwanyi, the queen. They ask for the goddess's blessings and anoint me with palm oil. I promise myself in service to the people.

Zirachi tells me that once the troubles are past and Udo is removed from power, we'll have a proper coronation in front of all Kun. There will be music, food, and celebration for days—even greater than the New Yam Festival. The traditional red cap of the Eze will be placed on my head.

I can barely imagine it.

My thoughts and memories are still a jumble, confusing and strange. There are moments I feel at ease with myself and times when everything feels unfamiliar and new. Amara and Chizoba. Their memories, likes, dislikes, mannerisms, and everything else that made them unique is all mixed up into something new—me.

I notice that people look at me differently too. As I walk the corridors of the temple, I see the sidelong glances and catch whispers between apprentices, and even among some of the griots. Yes, there is hope and joy. The binding means the long-awaited restoration of Kun is possible. But there is also fear. People move more slowly around me. Their actions are more deliberate, the way one might act if there were a dangerous animal nearby.

Most frustrating of all, even though I have magic, I haven't been able to show it. The council decided that Uchendu would begin private instruction with me, and I've spent hours with him. We talk about the powers that other earth children before me have displayed and what my powers might be.

"You have the ability but lack the knowledge," Griot Uchendu says. "Conjuring comes most easily to those who are connected to the earth and its power. Oala's power. Even then, it takes skill and practice to use it. Sometimes we learn best in the act of doing. I can feel magic in you. It will come out when the time is right."

I don't want to doubt the griot, but I feel like he might as well be speaking another language.

Griot Uchendu picks up a plant that is on the table.

"Let us start small. Nature can camouflage. One needs no trinkets or magicked cloaks if you can allow the earth to hide you." He puts his hand on the glossy green leaves of the plant, and slowly I see a change come across his skin. Dark green leaches into his brown fingers until his hand is the same shade as the plant. Next, leaves and stems ink themselves into this green palette. Soon, his hand is undistinguishable from the plant beneath it.

"You must concentrate on being part of the plants, trees, grasses—the world around you. Quiet your mind and think only of blanketing yourself with nature."

The griot removes his hand, and I see the color fade until it is as it was before. I put my own hand out and concentrate. At first nothing happens, but as I concentrate harder, a pinprick of green rises in the center of my hand and begins to creep outward like a spider. I gasp and pull my hand back. It returns to its warm brown color.

"Try again," he encourages. "Don't be afraid."

I hold out my hand once more and concentrate. My heart beats fast, and I press my eyes together. When I open them, my hand is still its ordinary brown.

"You have to concentrate and clear your mind of fear to keep the covering in place," Griot Uchendu says kindly, "but that was good start. It took my apprentice Mataye several months to manage to cloak even a finger—" He stops. No one has seen Mataye since the day of the binding. It seems impossible that he was involved, but his absence is his testimony. Uchendu continues, "See here. This is proof that magic is in you, Amarachi. You only need claim it."

During our practice sessions, Uchendu takes out his kora and sings to me about kings and queens of the past. My sisters and brothers. Those like Eze Ikemba and Eze Nwanyi Adaobi, the first queen. All Oala's children have the ability to make plants grow. Where they step, the earth becomes fertile. Where they breathe, food is bountiful and sweet. This is what the kingdom needs now, but there are other powers, special ones, that some heirs possess. Some can move earth—rock, sand, mud, or clay—and shape it to any form. Uchendu sings of how heirs of the past used their powers to erect the first castles and temples of Kun.

Other songs tell of earthquakes that could shake enemy strongholds and great crevasses that would swallow armies. These powers show themselves when Kun is under threat and the kings and queens need to lead their people into battle.

But despite my attention and efforts, my training moves slowly.

No heir before me has been split and rebound, and I know Uchendu is concerned.

Some days, Griot Uchendu asks me to accompany him on a walk, and we talk. I enjoy our conversations and the chance to leave the confines of the temple. One afternoon, we go across the lake to the forest. The drought is beginning to show. He bends down and strokes the leaves of a bitter leaf sapling languishing in a dusty patch of ground.

"Look at this plant," he says. "Can you help it?"

"How?" I ask.

"Place your hand on the earth and let your mind explore. Find out what it needs."

Squatting next to the griot, I run my fingers

through the dust around the bitter leaf. "There is no life besides this seedling," I say slowly. "There should be more to support it, but it is gone. No minerals, no moisture. The ground is compact, and the plant has no way to spread its roots," I say.

"Do you sense how to make it better?" Uchendu asks quietly.

I think quietly, then reach and pick up a few rocks. "There are nutrients here," I say, rolling the stones in my palm, "but they need to be released."

"Can you do that?" the griot continues.

I concentrate on the two rocks in my hand. I feel them grow warm and vibrate. Tiny cracks spider across their surfaces but then stop.

"Your magic will reveal itself in time," he says gently. We rise and eventually return to the temple.

As we approach the main hall, an apprentice walks up to us quickly.

"Teacher," he says, "a scout has just returned from Benta and wishes to report to the council. The others are assembling."

"Thank you," Uchendu replies. "Amarachi, you should come. It is time you learn about the state of your kingdom."

In the great hall, I see several griots seated around the large table. Uchendu escorts me to the head of the table, to the chair that had been his. "Sit here, my dear," he says. Once I sit, he takes the seat to my right. I look over and see Zirachi coming and jump up to greet her.

"Zirachi, where have you been today?" I ask. "Will you stay with me?"

"Of course," she says, walking back with me to the table. I sit down again, but Zirachi lingers behind.

"Please, sit with us," Griot Uchendu says. Zirachi smiles warmly and takes the seat to my left.

Okwu enters with Ndidi. I have not seen him for several days, and I wonder if he has been the one gathering information from Benta.

"Eze Nwanyi. My queen," he says, bowing to me. He grins at Zirachi, who shakes her head. It feels strange to be referred to as "queen" by anyone, and even stranger to hear it from Okwu.

"I bring a report of Eze Udo's movements in the city," Okwu says. "My part in the queen's escape has been discovered, so I could not openly return, but I spoke to the Nkume that remain faithful to the griots. I confirmed that Eze Udo is amassing a great army. With the attack on Queen Amarachi unsuccessful, he is not going to waste the information he has been given. Eze Udo knows how to find this temple, and they are marching toward us now.

They will be here by daybreak."

Murmurs echo around the room. Uchendu holds up his hand. "How many does Udo bring?" he asks.

"The Nkume is five hundred warriors strong. He has another two hundred guards and tower sentries and will bring them as well. The Ugha total near one hundred."

We are wildly outnumbered. Uchendu raises his hand again. "Then the time has come," he says, looking at me.

"Time for what?" I ask.

"To see if you can harness your magic against the enemies of Kun."

I panic. "I'm not ready!" I exclaim.

Griot Uchendu puts his hand on mine. "It is all right, child. The goddess will help us."

"And I won't leave your side," says Zirachi.

I still feel queasy. I know how brutal Eze Udo can be. He wants to kill me, and now he is desperate enough to take any risk.

"Queen Amarachi has already had one attempt on her life," Okwu says, "and does not need to risk another. There are fighters from the city who will come to our aid. She should not be put in harm's way."

"I agree," says Zirachi, standing up and addressing the group. "She is a child and has no business near a battle of any kind. Our responsibility is to protect her."

"And we will," says Griot Ndidi, walking to Zirachi's side and taking her hand.

"Our solemn duty has always been to protect the earth child," Uchendu says firmly. "The battle will be difficult, but it is one we must win. The future of Kun is in the balance."

My family, Griots Uchendu and Ndidi, and so many others are willing to sacrifice themselves for me. I feel relief at the griot's words but also guilt. The weight of responsibility, of being queen, feels heavy for the first time. Okwu and Zirachi will fight, and I'm supposed to be able to protect them. But I can't. I feel as small and powerless as I felt back on the road from Danel.

Once the defense plan is decided, people rush to prepare for the siege. They amass rocks to hurl over the walls, ready bows and quivers containing arrows, and barricade doors to keep out Udo's forces. The griots use their voices and instruments to spin protective enchantments across the island, melodies to slow the enemy's approach and turn nature against the would-be intruders.

I want to help, but I only get in the way. Even Nweke is given tasks to help the griots. Instead,

Lebechi and I sit together in my room.

Something holds me back, a door that I have yet to unlock. Like the dream I had of my tower, when I was Amara; I still need to find the key to unlock my destiny.

CHAPTER 21

MOTHER OF ALL

In the late hours of the night, I wake up suddenly. I lie in bed listening to quiet breathing from where Zirachi and Lebechi lie sleeping on their mats. The temple is silent except for the rush of the wind outside my window. As I stare up at the ceiling, my fears for the dawn swirl in my brain. The hunter comes closer, and I am cornered.

I absentmindedly touch my neck and think of my birthmark. For so long, it's been something that I've wanted to hide. A mark of shame. Now my world has turned upside down. The little crescent is not a curse but a sign that I have been blessed.

I sit up in bed. *Blessed!* I have been so focused on learning about my past that I have forgotten something essential. Something that might help me connect to my powers.

One person has the answers I need. My mother, the goddess Oala.

I get out of bed, careful not to wake Zirachi and Lebechi, and creep to the door. There are voices coming from the great hall, but I see no one in the corridor.

I slip out before anyone can stop me. Shadows play off the walls as I silently run down the passageway. Each footstep or murmured voice makes me stop, and my heart pounds. At last, I come to the door and push.

Every home in Kun has an altar to Oala, but in this place it is more than a simple table—it is a sanctuary. Moonlight glints through the high window and casts milky light into the room. It is an enormous shrine to the goddess—larger and more beautiful than the mbari shrines in my village. Red, yellow, black, white. Rich colors and geometric patterns adorn the walls and the earthen pillars that tower above each corner of the room. The quiet beauty of the space reminds me that Oala is the patron of our people's creativity and art.

Painted statues of the goddess show her in all her glorious forms. A mother balancing a child on her knee. A warrior brandishing her sword. A kneeling woman preparing the dead to return to the earth. Wooden figures of animals and people dot the other areas, all facing toward the center of the room.

Candles flicker on the altar before me. Yams, a symbol of Oala's bounty, rest next to a coiled python, the messenger of the goddess. I think of the snake I encountered in the forest. The prayer mat leads me to kneel, and I trace with my fingers its intricately woven designs of kola nuts, leopard spots, the winding path of a serpent.

I close my eyes and breathe, listening to the sounds of the night. Into the stillness I speak. "Oala, I want to know who I am."

At first there is nothing, but then vibrations rumble the floor. Light surrounds me and becomes so bright, I raise my hands. When it fades, I open my eyes.

A tall woman stands before me. She has dark skin, black hair, and warm brown eyes. Her braids are twisted into an elaborate crown, and she wears a flowing robe of white. Her bright eyes are welcoming.

"My daughter," she says. Her words sound not only in my ears, but within my head, as if spoken from inside of me.

"Mother?" I ask while rising to my feet.

"I am Oala, mother to all, but you that I sent into

the world are most precious to me."

She walks toward me and wraps me in her arms. I feel like I am floating in the softest cotton, but there is strength. It reminds me of climbing in the orchard and finding the perfect branch from which to sit and view the world.

"I am so sorry for the world you have come into. Of all my children, your arrival has been the most troubled. Never since the days of the first kings and queens has Kun been in such despair. The False One creates a grave wound that will not soon be healed. You should have been raised with more knowledge of your powers, and of me. Now you must do your best to learn."

I look at the goddess. "I don't know how to defeat Udo—or restore Kun. Everyone tells me that I have great power, but I'm just a girl. I can't raise a blade of grass, let alone stop an army."

"You can. My strength rests inside you. It does not come from fierceness, or the desire for power or to inflict pain. Your power comes from love. You are the caretaker of my creation and the one who will resurrect it. The people are separate and broken now. When you embrace who you are and let go of fear, your power will come, and you will unite the kingdom."

"I'm scared."

Oala beckons with her hand, and I see the soft glow of a light. Another figure steps forth, an old man wrapped in dazzling robes. He is slight in build and has brown eyes that twinkle. Upon his head sits the crown of Kun. I recognize him from the floating images that come alive during Uchendu's songs. It is Ikemba, the last king.

"Amarachi," he says. "I wish I could have met you in life. Much of the strife of this moment would have been avoided, but alas, it was not to be. I prepared for your arrival and trusted the boy that I had raised to be your ally and regent. Though I loved him as a son, I could not leave him the crown. He was resentful, and so he sought to take what was not meant for him."

"How can I stop him now?"

"He may not listen to reason," says the king, "but remind him of his past. He was reared to be a man of honor. To respect the old ways. Perhaps there is something of that in him still. If anyone can kindle it, it is you."

The old king puts his hand on my cheek. "Sweet child—there is so much hardship before you. Being the queen is a difficult responsibility, but it will be the highest honor of your life. Take care of our people. They are good and deserve more than what has been left to them. Right the wrongs and unite our kingdom."

King Ikemba's hand drops, and he fades like mist into the night.

"I know my destiny," I say to Oala.

She smiles. "I am proud of you, Amarachi. You will be a great queen."

Out the window, I see that night has quietly turned to gray and dawn is coming.

"Good fortune to you my daughter, Queen Amarachi of Kun. May your rule be long, and may our people prosper. We will reunite on the other side but know that you have my strength and favor."

A rising translucence transforms Oala to nothing more than air and light. In a heartbeat, she is gone.

When I look down, the prayer rug has sprouted into a blanket of flowers—yellow trumpets like the ones Ebele gave me so long ago. I kneel and put my nose in their petals. Their fragrance is sweeter than honey. I joyfully run my fingers along the tops of the blooms and glimpse what I could bring back to the world.

A shrill horn trumpets in the distance, and I realize

167

with horror that Udo's army has arrived. Through the window, a blood-red sun creeps over the horizon and seems to light the world on fire.

I run headlong toward my room, and my heart pounds with my feet. The siege has started.

CHAPTER 22

THE BATTLE BEGINS

Outside the shrine, the temple is a tumult of shouts and pounding feet. I shrink against the wall, making myself as small as possible, but I know I can't stay here.

"Amarachi! Where are you?" Zirachi races down the hall, frantically searching and holding Lebechi by the hand. When she sees me, she runs over and wraps me in her arms. "What are you doing here?"

"I went to the shrine to pray," I say, my voice sticking in my throat.

She hugs me tighter, then says, "We will need those prayers. Come, the griots have ordered us to the upper battlements in case the walls are breached." She takes both our hands and we run down the hall until we reach the stairs.

We climb as fast as we can. Griots and apprentices pass us carrying weapons and shields. Through the slitted windows, I see the far shore is lined with soldiers dragging equipment, preparing to attack the temple. I keep running.

At the top of the last flight, we exit onto the battlements. As I look over the walls, a sudden swoop in my stomach overwhelms me. I crouch and put my head against the rough wall, waiting for the feeling to subside. The ground seems to jump around beneath me.

Lebechi wraps her small arms around me, and her warmth is calming. I lift my head.

"Stay here," Zirachi says to us, then she runs over to the griots who line the walls.

I pull myself up so I can peek over the edge and finally can see the whole awful scene. If Okwu had thought Udo would bring only seven or eight hundred warriors, he was gravely mistaken. I am sure there are more than a thousand soldiers stationed along the lake and at the edge of the forest. The image of Eke the python whips in the air on the royal banner. I narrow my eyes in anger. How dare this king continue to hide behind my mother's symbol and name!

Eze Udo emerges from the trees and walks to

the river's edge. To the naked eye, it appears that he looks upon a vast, empty lake, but he knows the truth. Someone brings him a speaking horn, and his voice booms across the water.

"We have come to accept your surrender! Turn over the earth child, and no harm will come to anyone. Disobey, and we will knock your temple to the ground."

From somewhere below me, I hear Griot Uchendu's voice echo loudly from the temple.

"We are servants of Oala. You have claimed a throne to which you have no right! The people may not remember, but we do."

Eze Udo laughs. "I have been patient with your interference, but no more."

He beckons, and the Ugha line the shore. The women and men of his contingent raise their arms and begin to chant. Drummers beat loudly on ikoro drums to the rhythm of their voices. As the Ugha speak, the veil around the temple falls and the water churns. Stones emerge on the lake, but this time it is not just a few. The whole bottom of the lake rises up. They crash together in a patchwork of rock. The water sinks below, leaving at last a muddy surface for Udo's army to cross.

With a thunderous roar, the Nkume rush forward.

The archers on the battlements let loose a volley of arrows. The Nkume put up their shields. Some arrows find their mark, but the king's guard continue their attack. My heart pounds as the soldiers eventually reach our shore.

Another volley of arrows flies. Zirachi and others begin to rain stones down on the attackers. The thud of stones upon bodies makes me shudder, but it does not stop the Nkume and Ugha as they run for the main doors. Three Ugha thrust their arms at the doors and begin battering it with their cries, their voices harsh and dissonant. The griots on the battlements try to stop them, using their voices to hurl sharp blasts of sand from the shore. The three retreat, and another group starts an attack on the walls themselves, trying to loosen brick and clay.

I am so focused on the action below me that I forget to pay attention to the shore. As I look across the water, I see Eze Udo himself striding across the stone lake. He does not intend to watch the battle from afar. As more of his people cross, I see how overwhelming the odds are for us.

A great crack echoes in my ears, and Lebechi and I scream as the whole temple shakes. The walls below us blast open. Before Udo's forces can move forward, a loud cry emerges from within, and the griots and apprentices run out. Okwu leads the charge.

"People of Kun! Fight for Oala! Fight for our kingdom!" he screams. "Brothers and sisters of the Nkume, you know I speak truth. Show to whom your true loyalty lies!" Ndidi and others echo his cries, and the air fills with the rhythm of drums and more.

There is great commotion. For a moment, warriors who had arrived with Udo's forces hesitate; miraculously, some turn and block their former comrades, crossing swords with their own.

On the edge of the forest, it is the same. Nkume, hearing Okwu call, turn their weapons and begin to fight back against Eze Udo.

The battle grows heated as griots and soldiers fight on each side. Shouts and the clank of swords ring in the air. The tide of the battle has turned.

Looking below again, I see Eze Udo step onto our rocky shore. He scans the scene, and he strides toward the fallen door. At the threshold, his way is blocked. Griot Uchendu steps forward.

"Move aside, old man," says Eze Udo. "I will have the girl."

"You shall not," replies the older man. "You have defiled the sanctity of our temple and betrayed your vows as protector of the queen—vows that all of the regents before you have honored."

Udo raises his sword and swings it through the air. Uchendu dodges, but the Eze swings again. Uchendu lifts his voice and rapidly plucks the strings of the small lute he holds. A pulse of light shoots toward the king. Udo raises his sword to shield himself, then swings again. The old griot staggers back off balance and falls to the ground.

Eze Udo approaches, but Uchendu is slow to get up.

"Stay here!" Zirachi yells at me, as she and others run down the stairs to join the fight below. Lebechi begins to whimper in my arms, but I can't tear my eyes away from what is happening.

The king lifts his sword into the air and aims it at Uchendu.

"No!" I scream as I rise from my hiding place. I lean forward and my hands tingle. Not just words leave me but power. The ground vibrates with my cry, and people stumble and fall. "No!" I scream again.

The earth around Eze Udo cracks, and bricks from the temple fall in chunks, sending Udo's people running.

The tremors ripple out across the lake and shake the very trees in the forest. The vibrations loosen the stones on the battlements, and I feel myself falling forward. It's as if I am flying. Soaring above the griots, the Nkume, my fear.

"No!" I command one last time. I fall toward the earth and what I imagine will be a quick and certain death.

But it doesn't come. I feel another surge of power, and the earth rises to greet me. I am enveloped in pillowy clouds of dust. I see nothing in the swirl of clay and sand until, at last, I collapse hard, but safely, on the ground.

I test my body, making sure nothing is broken, then rise slowly. I hear a voice.

"Hello, little queen," says a man. I turn toward Mataye, now wearing the clothing of the Ugha. Several Nkume guards surround me as well. "It's good to see you again."

CHAPTER 23

CAPTURED

I try to scramble back toward the temple, but it is no use. Hands on my legs and arms tug me back.

"You are ours," says Mataye when I am roughly turned toward him. I kick and punch to get away from the man. My skin crawls at his closeness.

"We trusted you!" I shout at him. But there is nowhere to go. An Nkume guard has each of my hands and I cannot escape. "You were supposed to help us, but you lied. You poisoned me!" Hot tears burn my cheeks.

"I did what was right," Mataye replies. "I spent years with the griots and finally saw the truth. They are chained to the past. They follow traditions that keep our country bound to the whim of someone like you. Who are you to tell us we cannot rule our own?"

"But I *am* your own," I say, standing straight. "If you learned nothing in your studies, then you are a poor student. I understand more than you ever will. Oala is mother of all, and a kingdom cannot be built on might. A ruler must work for the good of their people. That is how we thrive. Eze Udo and you who follow him are driving our home to dust. You don't care that people are starving as long as you have power. I will stop you."

My cheeks are hot, and I glare at those around me. Harsh clapping draws my attention, and the crowd near the sound parts. Eze Udo approaches, slapping his hands together heartily, though his face holds no mirth.

"A pretty speech, child." He looks at me as though I'm an insignificant insect to be squashed.

"Your words are noble. One would think you had been raised in the palace instead of a rat's nest in Danel or that forsaken tower."

I struggle to free myself from the grip of the soldiers who hold my arms, but I cannot.

"I have learned what it means to be brave and noble," I say. "I learn it from everyone who fights against you. From my mother, Zirachi; from Okwu;

from those Nkume who turned against you during the battle. Uchendu risked his life to protect me. Chizoba trusted me, and Amara sacrificed all for someone she loved. They have taught me what it means to be a leader."

Udo listens, but the hatred in his eyes only burns more intensely. "Sacrifice? I sacrificed too. For years, I followed the teachings of the griots who instructed me in my duties as regent. The king treated me as a son, but I was not good enough to be his heir."

He spits on the ground and turns to his soldiers. "When the king began to ail, I took over more responsibilities, and I realized that there was no reason I could not continue. I was able to rule—indeed, I was doing so.

"I asked the king why we followed the old ways so blindly. But I forgot what he was. Oala's child. Nothing I could say would sway him. I was merely a tool that served a useful purpose, to be thrown away when a replacement arrived."

"Your name means *peace*, but you've brought the opposite to Kun," I say.

"This kingdom will have peace, and I will lead it," Udo says to me. "There is nothing that you, girl, or anyone else can do to stop me. You may have magic, but not control. That is helpful to me."

I continue to struggle, frustration bubbling inside me. Eze Udo is right. I have the power to free myself, but I'm unable to use it yet.

"I will end this now," Udo says quietly.

He waves his hand, and guards bring several people into the circle. I gasp.

Zirachi is covered with scrapes but raises her chin in defiance. Okwu also is battle-worn and bloodied, but he stands straight before the king. Lastly, Uchendu is dragged forward. Despite an oozing gash on his temple, his face carries such serenity. His gaze settles on me, and despite my fear, I too feel his quiet assurance. I look for Ndidi, but I don't see her.

"The warriors who turned against me have fled," Eze Udo says. "I will hunt them down. As an end to this treachery, we will execute you rebels in the city square in Benta. It is you who have upset the peace of our realm and kept my attention away from the needs of those who are suffering. When you are gone, the people will see how much better off we are without the shackles of the old ways."

"What you do is an abomination to the goddess. The chains you seek to put on others," Uchendu says slowly, his voice a rasp, "are the ones that will bind you."

"Your time is done, old man. A new sun rises on

Kun, and you will not stand in my way."

Soldiers drag the others. I try to run to Zirachi, but I cannot break the iron grips on my arms.

"Hold fast, Amarachi," Zirachi shouts back.

Eze Udo walks back and surveys me again with disdain. "I will dispose of you first," he says. "In front of all those you claim to love. They will see that you are not worth the faith they put in you. What hope is left inside them will be crushed."

He nods to his soldiers, and I too am dragged after the rest.

CHAPTER 24

FINAL STAND

I huddle in the corner of my cell and wonder how I have come to this.

As Amara, I was raised as a poor girl with little that was special about me, but I was happy. As Chizoba, I also had my moments of light and love. Now the weight of the world seems to rest on my shoulders, and I don't know what to do.

I have the power to right what is wrong, but I still don't know how to use it. Because of me, three other people are scheduled to die. Three people who have helped me and who I care about with all my heart. They first will watch Eze Udo execute me and take the powers that I have not yet been able to harness.

In despair, their own deaths will follow. And all will be lost.

"Zirachi," I call into the dank air. We can't see or touch each other, but we have the moment to talk.

"Yes, my love," Zirachi responds. I notice that Zirachi has changed since our journey began. Once sparing with her affection, even though I knew how she felt, now my mother speaks with her emotion plain. I think it has something to do with Okwu coming back, knowing how close she has again come to losing the people she loves.

"I'm sorry. Nothing happens, though I am trying to use my magic. I'm a failure as queen."

"Hush," Zirachi soothes. "Don't say that."

"Aye," Okwu's deep voice replies. "Strength comes in many forms, and I watched you stand up to Eze Udo today. Only a queen could have done so."

"They are right," Uchendu says. "Magic may not come soon enough for our lives to be spared, but that is no fault of yours. Have faith that when the time is right, Oala will free the people from the yoke Udo has put on them."

"I hope it's so."

"Amarachi, you were not in your room when the battle started. Where were you?" Uchendu asks.

I wipe my eyes. "I prayed at the shrine." I hesitate

and then add, "I saw Oala."

"That is a great gift," Uchendu says. "She rarely appears, even to her own children."

I remember the warmth of Oala's robes and the tree trunk strength of her arms. Somewhere inside me, those exist as well. "She told me she was proud of me," I say.

"As are we all," says Zirachi.

Loud clanking shatters the quiet, and soldiers march into the dungeon. They unlock the cells and order all four of us out.

The sun has risen, and the sky is a mix of orange and red above the horizon. Despite the early hour, the city square is full of people, an apparent edict from the Eze. They line the road as we're escorted from the castle to the platform at the other end of the square.

The ground of the market is paved with stone, and before the platform loom three large wooden posts. The guards roughly lead each of the others to a post and bind them with rope. I am led to steps that take me to the top of the platform. I look down on the other three from where I am forced to stand, my hands bound behind me. We wait. The sun burns off the color of the dawn and hints at the heat of the coming day.

I squint through the bright light toward the castle. There's movement on the balcony across from the platform. Eze Udo comes out in full regal garb instead of battle armor. He wears the traditional red cap and eagle feather that denote his status as Eze. Clearly, he means our executions to be symbolic—an ending of challenges to his reign.

"People of Kun, you come here today to witness the end of an era. For too long, we've been shackled to the rule of people unlike ourselves. Kings we didn't choose and others who've perpetuated their tyranny. King Ikemba raised me as his son. When he died, he charged me to protect the kingdom until another who was fit to rule had come. I see no other fit to rule. For the good of our kingdom, I sentence these before you to death."

"I would speak!" I shout into the morning air. The crowd turns from the balcony to me. Udo's angry glare is also aimed at me, but I don't waver.

In the distance, I hear a sound. The gentle strumming of a kora. I'm not a griot, but I have power in my words and will make the people listen.

"Eze Udo says that you must be ruled by someone like you, chosen by the people and not by Oala. What he doesn't tell you is that he is neither," I shout at the crowd. The notes of the kora rise and fall, becoming louder and more insistent. Other instruments join our song.

"Do you try to kill innocent children? Do you burn homes and drag people from their farms? If you do, then yes, you are like Udo. But I think you're not." My mouth is dry, but I continue. "Eze Udo is ruthless. His only desire is power. He says that King Ikemba put the mantle of leadership on him, but that's a lie. Udo was supposed to be a caretaker, not a king. He's thrust himself into this position and will do anything to hold on."

I notice that Udo has left the balcony, and some of his soldiers are moving toward the platform. I speak more quickly. Griots who are playing koras, balafons, karinyas, and drums push their way through the crowd. I see Ndidi, her face alight as she sings to the sky. The music weaves around me—through me. It gives me strength, and the people are transfixed by my words.

"He also says that he wants Kun to have a leader chosen by the people. Have any of you chosen him to lead you—or have you been forced to accept him? Since he took the throne, our nation has been dying. People are starving, and the ground turns to dust. Food is scarce, and families separate as they try to keep their children alive. This is because of Eze Udo."

Udo walks into the city square, flanked by his guards. "Silence her!" he shouts to the soldiers standing below the platform.

The music rises in a crescendo. People turn and whisper to one another, their eyes wide.

"Amanye!" some say. "It is true!" Their voices respond to the song of the griot. An agreement. A challenge to the king. "Amanye!" they say louder.

They are remembering.

"I stand before you as the rightful ruler of Kun!" I shout with all that is in me. "I am Oala's child, born twelve years ago, who should have been brought to the palace and crowned. Instead, Udo tries to kill me. He has failed before, but he will do it again today in front of you all. Do not allow him to succeed. The life of our kingdom is at stake!"

Nkume guards grab me and wrestle me down. Ugha strike the griots who are performing, yanking their instruments away and dashing them to the ground. The people continue to shout, "Amanye!" but are being drowned out by Eze Udo's drums and the clank of swords.

As my face lies against the rough clay of the square, tears sting my cheek. I've told the truth. Even if the people can't stop what is about to happen, they know.

"A brave speech," says the king, "but my people

186

will not be fooled by your lies." He looks at the crowd, and the people shrink back. I see that they don't believe him, but with a falling heart, I also see that they're too afraid to do more than watch.

"It is time to punish the traitors," Udo says. "You were to be first, Amarachi, as proof to the others that they cannot force a false queen on us." He smiles, but no one returns his mirth. "Instead, I think these three should go first. You spoke rashly, and you should know the pain that rash words can cause."

Udo raises his arms, and a row of archers quickly assemble in front of the posts. They lock eyes on their targets and draw their bows taut.

"Don't do this!" I shout as the guards pull me to the side where I will see every arrow hit its target.

"Away!" Udo says.

The archers' fingers release the bowstrings, and the arrows slice through the air, aimed for each prisoner's heart. Hearts I love.

Without warning, the ground between the archers and the targets churns and a wall of clay shoots to the sky. The arrows snap as they strike. People in the market scream and run. The earth trembles again and the posts that had stood firm sink into a bubbling mass of mud. The prisoners wobble, but as soon as the posts disappear into the ground, they're able to step out of the ropes that had held them moments before.

I turn to those holding my arms. "Let me go." My voice reverberates with power. They lose their hold and regroup with the other soldiers.

"Take them!" Eze Udo screams, but I'm not afraid of him anymore. I finally understand my power, and it doesn't come from study or thinking. It comes from feeling. Protecting and caring for others.

I move into the chaos and try to find the others. I spot them across the square and run toward them. The glint of metal catches my eye, and I see Eze Udo running toward me, sword held high.

I raise another shield of dirt between us, knocking Eze Udo backward and covering myself with crumbling earth. I continue to run.

"Here," Zirachi calls. I dart toward a group of carts where Zirachi and Uchendu crouch with Ndidi. "Are you all right?" Zirachi asks, touching my face and arms, looking for any sign of injury.

"I'm fine, but it's not safe." I see that a true battle has erupted. The warriors Okwu led have snuck into the city with the crowds and are now fighting Udo's guards. With surprise, I also realize that some citizens are fighting with them using whatever makeshift weapons they can find. Udo's soldiers are no longer in the majority. "We can make it to the gate if we hurry," I say. Zirachi nods.

"Father, can you walk?" Ndidi asks.

"I am an old man, but yes, I think I can," he says with a hint of a smile.

She helps him stand up. When we see an opening, I whisper, "Go!"

We have gone only a few steps into the open when Udo runs across the courtyard. He has traded his sword for a spear. With a bellow, the Eze hurls his weapon.

I thrust out my hand, and there is a terrible roar from the earth. The ground before me cracks, and a huge fissure spreads like an axe has cleaved through the earth. Fighters on both sides of the chasm stumble back so as not to be swallowed.

Unable to stop his momentum, Udo falls screaming into the gaping mouth of the earth. To Oala's domain.

I turn, expecting to feel the spear pierce my chest, but instead I am pushed. Okwu shields my body with his own. "No!" I scream as he crumples on top of me.

I gently slide him onto his side and look helplessly at his dirt-streaked face.

"Why did you do that?" I cry.

"Because the kingdom needs you."

"But we need *you*."

Zirachi drops to the dusty ground. She carefully pulls the spear from her brother's side, causing Okwu to cry out in pain. I lean over him, wetting Okwu and the ground with the tears I can no longer control.

I don't want to let go, even when I feel Zirachi's hand on my back. But I lift my head when Ndidi cries, "Look!" I turn to face whatever threat is next, but there's none. I see only . . . green. Where my tears have fallen, a small plant pushes through the trampled ground and spreads feathery leaves.

"I think it's obara," Ndidi whispers.

I watch in amazement as gentle stems sprout clusters of small white blossoms. The telltale fragrance of the obara blooms fill the air.

"It is!" Zirachi says with a gasp. "Thank Oala! This will stop the bleeding until we can reach a healer." She plucks the plant and crushes it in her palm, then gently places the bundle against Okwu's wound. He winces. Ndidi hands Zirachi a sash, which she uses to create a makeshift dressing to secure the healing plant in place.

After a few moments, Okwu gestures to Zirachi for help, and she props him up so he can look at me directly. "Zira told me that you're special, and now everyone else knows it too."

A crowd forms around us. Villagers and soldiers, griots, and farmers watch us. Zirachi carefully helps Okwu to his feet and beckons me to stand.

"Eze Udo is gone. There is no need for us to fight anymore. Amarachi is the rightful queen of Kun. All hail Amarachi!"

There is a roar of approval from the people, but I focus on none of it. I turn and bury my face into Zirachi's waist and receive the hug that I knew was there. The hug of a mother.

CHAPTER 25

TRUE QUEEN

The sun streams brightly through the windows of the throne room. I am still not used to living in the castle, not used to being called queen. But I will be soon. After Udo's defeat, many of his people heeded Okwu's words and asked to be pardoned for their actions. Though still recovering from his injury, Okwu advised me to show fairness and accept back those he trusted who wished to serve the new queen. For others, he advised banishment.

Nduka, Mataye, and the other Ugha have been exiled to the territory beyond the dust of the Zare and told never to return. I want no more bloodshed in Kun.

I walk over to the gallery where all the portraits

of the kings and queens of Kun hang. A new one, mine, was commissioned and hangs at the end, still covered by a cloth. I asked the artist to do something unusual and have kept it secret. The painting will be uncovered after the coronation.

"It's time," I hear a voice say. I turn to Zirachi. She looks different from our days on the farm, wearing the clothes of a lady instead of a farmer. Her dress today is of white linen, which looks beautiful against her brown skin and amber eyes, and colorful beads grace her arms and ankles. Her face is warm, and there is a light of happiness in her eyes.

"Ndidi sent me to fetch you. It will take some time to prepare you for your coronation, so we must hurry."

"I can hardly believe those words are meant for me," I say and then pause. "Do you ever miss the farm, Zirachi? Would you want to go back?"

Zirachi looks out the window and then back at me. "I don't think so. I loved the orchard, but I can grow trees here in the city. My parents left me that field and farm, but some memories are too painful. It seems right to start a new life here."

"Why did you take me in all those years ago?"

"Hmm . . ." Zirachi says with a smile, "that's a good question. It made no sense at the time, but I think it was the goddess at work. Okwu couldn't return, so he sent you instead. It's something for which I'll always be grateful to him. I don't think you could have made a wiser choice than making him your regent."

"The people trust him, and I do as well. He'll help me learn what I must to bring our kingdom back to health."

"Tell me, Eze Nwanyi. What do you want to do with this life you now have?"

"Well, I've learned from the mistakes of Udo, and perhaps also from oversights of my ancestors. I want to see our kingdom and let the people see me, but that is not enough. We are all children of Oala, each one of us. Udo gave the people no say, but I will. Each region of our kingdom will send their elders to Benta to represent them and share their needs. I think the kings and queens before spent too much time away from our brothers and sisters. I intend to change that."

Zirachi beams. "You're wise beyond your years, Amarachi. How can I help?"

"You've helped me already, Zirachi. Everything I am, I owe to you," I say, squeezing her hand.

"But there's work to be done first," I say. I walk over to a small table. A little hibiscus flower sits in a pot. "The dust storms have stopped, but it's time to repair our land—I finally understand how." I press my fingers to the dirt in the pot, and there's a change. The plant spreads its leaves and grows taller. New buds spring forth and bloom. In a moment, it goes from a single bloom to a glorious cascade of purple and gold.

"Beautiful," Zirachi breathes.

I smile. "Can I show you something?" I ask. "Everyone will see it later, but I want you to see it first."

I lead Zirachi to the gallery of the Eze and Eze Nwanyi of the past and stop before a covered painting. I reach up and pull the twisted rope, and the covering falls softly to the floor.

Within the gilt frame smile not one girl but two. Their hair is braided into twists, and each wears a royal crown and beautiful robes, the same that I will be wearing for my coronation ceremony. In the portrait, the girls sit close, holding hands in a bond of friendship. At the bottom, the portrait reads "Queen Amarachi" and below, in smaller letters, is written "In honor of Lady Amara and Lady Chizoba."

Zirachi wipes away a tear. "A beautiful tribute."

I nod. "The griots have prepared a praise song to be performed at the coronation in their honor—our honor. It might be hard for some to understand, but they are both a part of me. I can't separate our memories anymore, but I wouldn't be queen if it weren't for what both of them gave. Bravery, strength, and love. The people will remember them." I sigh. "I hope I'll be a good queen."

"You could not be anything but," Zirachi says. "Now, let us go, or Griot Ndidi will have my head."

Zirachi replaces the covering over the portrait, and we walk hand in hand up to the tower.

EPILOGUE

Amarachi
First among the stars
Protector of Kun

                              Amanye!

Bringer of life
Restoring our past
Driving out the one who forsook his name

Daughter of the earth
Oala's beloved
Ancestors praise your birth

                              Amanye!

Daughter of Zirachi

Blessed of women
The sapling nurtured became strong

Two became one
And became stronger than all
Praise to our queen

                                            Amanye!

Names are power
Ancestors give us strength
In knowing our names
We know ourselves

From kings and queens you come
Ikemba, strength of our nation
   and Adaeze, the princess
   from Anyaka, the bold
   and Ezeoha, the people's king
   through Ochi, whose laughter is good
   and Ikechi, Oala's strength
   Ndubisi, reminds you life is first
   and Awali, of your joy
From them and many more
Back to Madu the first
Born from the earth but
Of the people

Comes now, Amarachi
Oala's grace

                              Amanye!

Let the people remember
Let the people never forget

—Sung by Griot Nweke to Eze Nwanyi Amarachi
on the fiftieth anniversary of her coronation, Kingdom
of Kun

A NOTE FROM
THE AUTHOR

I have always been a lover of fairy tales.

When I was a child, my parents bought a set of books for my brother and me from a traveling salesman. My Book House, edited by Olive Beaupré Miller, included twelve hardcover volumes that started with *In the Nursery* in volume one and ended with *Halls of Fame* in volume twelve. The set is noted for being one of the first graded collections selected to meet the developing needs of young readers.

My favorite volumes were the middle books: *Through the Gates, Over the Hills,* and *Through the Fairy Halls.* In them I read and reread stories from the Brothers Grimm, Hans Christian Andersen, Charles Perrault, and many other tales passed down through various folk traditions.

Even though I loved the books, I did not find many stories with characters that were like me, a young Black girl. In fact, the only included story I clearly remember as seeming to connect to Black culture is the racially degrading tale of "Little Black Sambo" by Helen Bannerman. In the story, the titular character is given a fine set of clothes by his parents, Black Mumbo and Black Jumbo, and goes for a stroll in the jungle, where he soon meets a hungry tiger. I remember the story making me feel strangely uncomfortable as a child reader, but I didn't have the knowledge or context to understand why at that age.

Fast forward to 2015, when I began writing the novel that would become *Kingdom of Dust*. In my fifth-grade class, we were reading *The True Confessions of Charlotte Doyle* by Avi, a book about a young girl who, as the lone female passenger on a ship with a mutinous crew, transforms from a proper young lady to a hard-working sailor. To introduce the book, I found an empowering video about breaking gender stereotypes produced by the Always brand of Proctor & Gamble as part of their #LikeAGirl campaign.

In *Unstoppable*, girls are asked, "Have you ever been told that because you're a girl, you shouldn't do something?" A young girl responds, "I can't really, like, rescue anybody. It's, like, always the boys who rescue the girls in the stories."

Her answer inspired me to write a story where a

girl saves a princess in a tower—think "Rapunzel." And taking further inspiration from Disney's *Frozen*, I decided that the twist would be that, in the end, the girl saves herself.

The journey from that idea to a West African-inspired fantasy was a winding one. In my early drafts, the main character was a Black girl, but the setting was in a stereotypical medieval European landscape. I wanted to write the fairy tale I didn't have as a child, but my imagination was limited by my early diet of stories like the ones in the My Book House collection.

In 2018, I attended WriteOnCon, a virtual children's literature conference, and had a generous "red pencil" session with beloved middle grade author Gail Carson Levine. She shared feedback on my first pages and answered my questions about worldbuilding, character, and setting for almost an hour. One struggle I shared with her was that I didn't feel strongly connected to the medieval world I was creating. She said, "Medieval is a time period, though, not a place." That was my light bulb moment! I decided to "move" the story to Africa, and the world of Kun began to take shape.

For my novel *A Comb of Wishes*, I studied the connection between African griots and storytelling in the Black diaspora. In this book, I dug further into the role and importance of griots in West African society—and I gave them magic! Igbo mythology formed a starting place for my worldbuilding, and much of Kun springs from the wisdom and richness of the Igbo people and their culture. Their spirituality is seen in the connection the people of Kun have with each other, the earth, and the goddess Oala.

Kingdom of Dust has many themes. Memory, oral history, family, justice, and love. It's about learning from the past to preserve the future. But most importantly to me, it is a fairy tale.

A Black girl rescues a princess in a tower, and in doing so she saves not only the world, but herself.

GLOSSARY AND PRONUNCIATION GUIDE

Many words in *Kingdom of Dust* are based on the language of the Igbo people of southern Nigeria. Igbo is a *tonal* language, and words that are spelled the same may have different meanings based on their spoken tones. For example, "àkwà" means "bed," but "àkwá" means "egg." The word "chi" means "God" in Igbo, and it is a common prefix and suffix in names.*

In *Kingdom of Dust*, accents were omitted to make the book easier to read.

Akwete aa-KWAY-tey (Igbo): a traditional Igbo hand-woven cloth

Amanye ah-MAN-ye (Igbo): in choral responses, a traditional phrase of agreement meaning "it is true" or "indeed"

---

* Many of these names and meanings are found in *The African Book of Names: 5,000+ Common and Uncommon Names from the African Continent* by Askhari Johnson Hodari, PhD.

Arusi ah-RU-si (Igbo): spirits that are worshipped in the Igbo religion

Eke EH-keh (Igbo): python; also one of four Igbo market days

Eze EH-zeh (Igbo): king

Eze Nwanyi EH-zeh na-WAN-yi (Igbo): queen (woman king)

Griot GRI-oh (French): the traditional musicians, oral historians, and storytellers of West Africa

Mbari mm-BAH-ri (Igbo): a sacred house built to honor the earth goddess Ala, whose name means "ground"; a visual art form of the Igbo people

Nkume n-KUH-me (Igbo): rock

Ugha oo-GAH (Igbo): false

NAME PRONUNCIATIONS AND MEANINGS

Amara ah-MAH-ra (Igbo): grace

Amarachi ah-MAH-ra-chi (Igbo): grace of God

Chizoba chi-ZO-bah (Igbo): God protects us

Ebele eh-BEH-leh (Igbo): mercy, kindness

Ifeoma ee-FO-ma (Igbo): good thing; beautiful

Ikemba ee-KEM-bah (Igbo): strength of the nation

Lebechi leh-BEH-chi (Igbo): look unto God

Mataye mah-TAH-yeh (Nigerian/Igarra): only God is perfect

Mmesoma MEH-soma (Igbo): kindness

Ndidi n-DI-di (Igbo): patience

Nduka n-DOO-kah (Igbo): life is more important

Nweke n-WEH-keh (Igbo): born on Eke market day (one of four Igbo market days)

Oala o-AH-lah (Igbo): inspired by Ala, the earth goddess of the Igbo people

Okwu OK-wu (Igbo): word

Uchendu oo-CHEN-du (Igbo): mind is life

Udo oo-DOH (Igbo): peace

Zirachi zee-RA-chi (Igbo): ask God to do anything for you and He will

ACKNOWLEDGMENTS

To my mother, Lillie: You are a wonderful storyteller and one of the griots of our family. Thank you for your endless support.

Thank you to my brother, Dudley: You are always the first person in the family with whom I can share my ideas.

To my children, Michaela, Benjamin, and Althea: I love you! Thank you for keeping me inspired.

To my extended family: I'm so grateful for your support and love.

To my agent, Lindsay Auld, and the wonderful team at Writers House: Thank you for continuing to be my advocates and for supporting my creative work.

To Rosemary Brosnan: I'm so grateful for your editing vision and help in making this manuscript come alive. You always ask such helpful questions!

To the wonderful team at HarperCollins and Quill Tree Books, thank you for your support of my work: Courtney Stevenson, Rye White, Kerry Moynagh and the HarperCollins sales team, Patty Rosati, Mimi Rankin, David Curtis, and Robby Imfeld, and Taylan Salvati.

To Michael Machira Mwangi: I am so fortunate to have your art on the cover again. Thank you for bringing Amara alive for young readers.

To Gail Carson Levine: Your critique of my first pages was a turning point in my revision of the manuscript. Thank you for your generous feedback and encouragement!

Thank you to Laura Pegram and Kweli for your continuing support and celebration of my writing journey.

Thank you to my fellow authors of KidLit in Color, the Brown Bookshelf's Amplify Black Stories Cohort, Black Creators in KidLit, BosKidLit, Kindling Words, and to many others for your nurturing support.

To my friends and colleagues at the Winsor School, thank you for supporting my creative pursuits and generously uplifting my work. Thank you to my former colleagues at Kentucky Country Day School for continuing to cheer me on.

Thank you to my students for inspiring me every day. Keep writing! My special thanks to Siri Erlingsson for being a willing first reader and for sharing her thoughts on my manuscript related to Igbo culture.

In my research, I found the book *Griots and Griottes* by Thomas A. Hale particularly helpful in creating my vision of Kun's griots. I thank the author for his work.

ABOUT THE AUTHOR

Lisa Stringfellow writes middle grade fiction and has a not-so-secret fondness for fantasy with a dark twist. Growing up, she was a voracious reader, and books took her to places where her imagination could thrive. She writes for her twelve-year-old self, the kid waiting to be the brown-skinned hero of an adventure, off saving the world. Lisa's work often reflects her West Indian and Black southern heritage. She received the inaugural Kweli Color of Children's Literature Manuscript Award for a draft of her first novel, *A Comb of Wishes*, which was a Bram Stoker Award Finalist, an Indies Introduce Top Ten title, an Indie Next List selection, and a New England Booksellers Association Book Award Finalist. Lisa is a middle-school teacher and lives in Boston, Massachusetts, with her children and bossy cat.